Praise for Bharati Mukherjee's most recent novel, *Jasmine*

"[A] rich novel . . . *Jasmine* stands as one of the most suggestive novels we have about what it is to become an American."
The New York Times Book Review

"Engrossing . . . Mukherjee once again presents all the shock, pain and liberation of exile and transformation. . . . With the uncanny third eye of the artist, Mukherjee forces us to see our country anew."
USA Today

"Irresistible . . . Seeing ourselves as others see us is only one of the attractions of this beautifully controlled, multifaceted chronicle of an illegal immigrant from India who suspects a predestined fate but is determined to reinvent her life."
Detroit Free Press

"A beautiful novel, poetic, exotic, perfectly controlled."
San Francisco Chronicle

"Artful and arresting . . . Breathtaking."
Los Angeles Times Book Review

WIFE

Bharati Mukherjee

FAWCETT CREST • NEW YORK

A Fawcett Crest Book
Published by Ballantine Books
Copyright © 1975 by Bharati Mukherjee Blaise

Library of Congress Catalog Card Number: 86-95038-7

ISBN 0-449-22098-2

This edition published by arrangement with Houghton Mifflin Company

Manufactured in the United States of America

First Ballantine Books Edition: April 1992

For Bart and Bernard.
    And for Leonard Gordon,
    who wondered about
    Bengali wives.

Dimple: any slight surface depression.
Oxford English Dictionary

Part One

DIMPLE Dasgupta had set her heart on marrying a neurosurgeon, but her father was looking for engineers in the matrimonial ads. Mr. Dasgupta was an electrical engineer (he called himself a "high-tension" man) with the Calcutta Electric Supply Company, and lived in a narrow pink house on Rash Behari Avenue. His neighbors on either side were engineers. Dimple wanted a different kind of life—an apartment in Chowringhee, her hair done by Chinese girls, trips to New Market for nylon saris—so she placed her faith in neurosurgeons and architects. She fantasized about young men with mustaches, dressed in spotless white, peering into opened skulls. Marriage would bring her freedom, cocktail parties on carpeted lawns, fund-raising dinners for noble charities. Marriage would bring her love.

"It will be a short engagement," Mrs. Dasgupta said. "Life is hard enough for our Calcutta boys without the added burden of a long engagement." Dimple was happy about that decision; she thought of premarital life

3

as a dress rehearsal for actual living. Years of waiting
had already made her nervous, unnaturally prone to
colds, coughs and headaches. Wasted years—she was
twenty—lay like a chill weight in her body, giving her
eyes a watchful squint and her spine a slight curve.

"Why are you worrying?" Mrs. Dasgupta often
asked. "Just wait and see; your father will find you an
outstanding husband. But only if you stop frowning.
Frowning gives you wrinkles."

But Dimple could not help worrying as the weeks,
then months, slipped by and two weddings took place
farther down the block. She worried that she was ugly,
worried about her sitar-shaped body and rudimentary
breasts. Would the now-inevitable engineer—she visualized him in starched khaki pants and dark glasses, still
mustached, on a half-built bridge directing laborers—
be disappointed that she wasn't bosomy and fair like a
Bombay starlet? She thought of breasts as having des-
tinies of their own, ruining marriages or making for-
tunes.

"Stop worrying!" Mrs. Dasgupta consoled. "Worrying
makes them shrink!"

In her despair, Dimple took to reading ads in wom-
en's magazines and buying skin whiteners ("Be the col-
our you were meant to be") and an isometric exerciser
("In two weeks my figure developed 10 cms."). The
girls in the ads were her friends. Like her, they suffered
and wept, even if they were fair and busty.

Scene in College Common Room (Ladies Only)

OLD-FASHIONED GIRL with long hair:
    I love Ganesh so much but how can I tell him
    about my physical defect? How can I make

things right? Help me! Please! You're my best
friend.

CUTE MODERN GIRL with short hair:

Don't be so blue, Vimla! Anyone can turn a
molehill into a mountain!

OLD-FASHIONED:

You are cruel to tease me. Just because you
have big . . .

CUTE MODERN:

I *am* your best friend. Would I tease you? Why
don't you be like me? Wear THE CONCRETE
BRA—I do.

OLD-FASHIONED:

(Shaken) *You?* But I couldn't . . . I mean, they
don't . . . (Frowns) But Ganesh and I are getting married in a fortnight. He'll be furious
when he finds out I was fooling him.

CUTE MODERN:

(Hugging Vimla) Silly, you don't have to *tell*
him. Love is blind and what do men know
about our secrets? (Winks at reader) After all,
isn't it what *your* Dreamboat wants? Satisfac-
tion or money back.

Dimple would have liked to send for the Concrete
Bra but Mrs. Dasgupta was far too bosomy to be sym-
pathetic. "There'll be no stuffing and trussing in this
house," she said. "You must be satisfied with what
God has given you. But use it to your best advantage."
Instead she prescribed prebath mustard oil massages,
ground almond and honey packs, Ping-Pong, homeopathic pills and prayers to Lord Shiva, the Divine Husband. She tore Dimple's order form into very small
pieces. More weeks passed. Dimple's intractable body
reported no change.

In the first week of July she had to be rushed to the hospital with a sharp pain in her chest. She couldn't breathe or talk. But when the doctor asked her to show him where exactly she hurt, she couldn't locate it. She watched his mouth grow cruel and skeptical. He was only an intern in a dirty smock with smudges of blood around the buttons. He couldn't respect her pain: it raised no welts; it didn't bleed. He wasn't married. She would kill herself rather than marry a man like that.

Dimple spent four days in her hospital room, drowning in white: white metal tables and bed, white sheets, patched white window curtains. Residents and nurses in white checked the chart at the foot of the bed, thrust thermometers into her mouth, felt her pulse and joked among themselves. A nurse with yellow teeth, Christian by the look of her, gave her a little pink pill at ten every night, then gossiped about the other patients. People who vomited blood, had collapsed stomach walls, mouth cancers, kidney stones. The funniest stories were about a fat woman with heart trouble who couldn't be given shots because the needle wasn't long enough to go through the fat. At night she heard a burn victim scream ("A human torch!" the nurse said. "Would you believe it, she set fire to herself!"), and she envied that woman. In Dimple's dreams, she became Sita, the ideal wife of Hindu legends, who had walked through fire at her husband's request. Such pain, such loyalty, seemed reserved for married women. How much easier to suffer from burns, stones, growths; from diseases with precise, even dignified, names. Life should have promised more than this waiting in a hospital bed.

After five days, Dimple's pain and fever went away and she was brought home in a taxi by her parents. Mrs. Dasgupta read the illness as a sign; mysterious pains, headaches, nervous tics were Nature's ways of indicating a young woman's readiness for marriage. She herself had been brought from the sickbed for her orthodox ceremony, and had promptly returned to it when the ordeal was over. She urged Mr. Dasgupta to look more carefully at matrimonial advertisements.

In July there were power cuts almost every other day. Every morning Dimple sat on her bed waiting for the power cut. She turned on the lights and the ceiling fan and plugged in the radio so she would know when the power went.

Her bed was littered with half-opened books, their spines bent. They looked like corpses on a battlefield. She was supposed to be studying for university exams—in a notebook still open on the bed she saw she had written, in happier times, "The Rebellion of 1857 was the result of a thousand small annoyances. Rumours of cow fat on the bullet-casings was just the icing on the cake"—but all she could think of was the imminent power cut. Lizards scurried up the wall behind her bed; she wondered where they went in the dark of the power cut. Once she'd found a dead baby lizard in her pillowcase.

In the moments immediately after a power cut, when the street noises were sharp and distinct, she heard the boy next door scream in pain because of water in his head. She visualized his head as a giant balloon battered by the monsoon rains. When the power came back again, the boy's screams were drowned by the hum of the radio and the ceiling fan.

In the winter, when power cuts were less frequent, she would say it was not doing without electricity that she hated, but the waiting, the endless waiting.

* * *

It was still July, and it had been on the whole an odd day for Dimple: no toast for breakfast because of a gas shortage, a mystery chain letter in the morning mail that promised riches or threatened death, rumors that the university exams would be postponed indefinitely and a straight rejection from an outstanding matrimonial candidate.

At noon her best friend came over to repeat the rumors about the postponements of the university exams. Her name was Paramita Ray, but everyone called her Pixie. Pixie had heard it from a cousin who was a medical student and had been waiting for the last eighteen months to take his exams. She carried two Bengali novels and the latest *Filmfare*.

Pixie lived two houses away, above a radio store and a photographer's studio. In the display window of the studio there was a large print of Pixie holding a birdcage and staring dreamily at two lovebirds. Pixie said being photographed with a birdcage was better than being photographed with a peacock feather fan or a wilting bouquet. But she insisted it was not a matrimonial portrait. She was determined to fall in love; the portrait, if anything, might land her a job in an airline office on Chowringhee, business lunches on Park Street, a small part in a high-class film. Important people walked by the studio every day.

"Are you absolutely sure about the exams?" Dimple asked.

Pixie was too busy to answer because she was cutting out a color picture of Amitabh Bachchan ("He's the new Bombay Steve McQueen!") from the film magazine she had brought with her. "Let's open the window. There's not enough light in this room. I want you to see Amitabh in the best light." It was Pixie's opinion that Dimple did not take Hindi films seriously enough.

She stood on the high wooden bed which was pushed against the tightly shuttered window, jiggled the rusty latch and pushed the shutters outward. Then she exhibited the picture of the tall, shy-looking Amitabh holding hands with his very short, smiling Bengali wife, also an actress. "That's love," Pixie said.

"What rot!" Dimple said, very excited. "What bunkum!" She remembered having read those phrases in an English novel long ago; they alone seemed to express the intensity of what she felt. Love had to be more than film stars holding hands on a tear-stained page. She could say love was not this, or this other, and definitely not that. But its precise description eluded her. She was sure love would become magically lucid on her wedding day. Pixie was lucky, Dimple thought; Pixie did not understand about waiting, she did not worry about the dark unless it happened during a Hindi movie, or about the radio dropping pitch and then dying in midsentence unless it was playing a favorite song. Pixie did not know that reading novels, studying for exams, flipping through film magazines were strategies of waiting.

"I don't think your cousin knows what he's talking about," Dimple said.

Two days later, while she was memorizing passages from *The Doctrine of Passive Resistance* for the exams and thinking not of freedom fighters and fasting armies led by a balding, bespectacled old man but of herself at some future date, a good wife, a docile wife conquering the husband-enemy by withholding affection and other tactics of domestic passive resistance, Mr. Dasgupta brought her a clipping from the morning paper:

Calcutta University officials disclosed yesterday that B.A. and B.Sc. examinations (Part One) will probably be postponed by several weeks.

On that day Dimple did something she had not done before. She opened the window behind her bed, picked up *The Doctrine of Passive Resistance* and lobbed it through the wrought-iron grille into the backyard. Without a B.A. she'd never get a decent husband. Couldn't those Calcutta University officials, who postponed exams and held up degrees as though they were nothing more important than cricket matches, be made to understand? All the handsome young engineers would be married by the time she got her degree.

She grew bitter during the last days of August, especially bitter about relying on others. Her father still circled ads for "the ideal boy"; he talked on the phone with the forced, conspiratorial gaiety of a desperate man trying to bargain. Her mother still ground almonds on a stone slab. No one would marry an ugly girl like her; no one would make her happy or treat her with respect. ("Don't be silly," said Mrs. Dasgupta. "Only Christians become spinsters.") One evening after the admission that a mechanical engineer residing in Germany had shown no interest in the discreet inquiries her father had made (hearing the word *Düsseldorf*, she had gone to a library and made a list of everyday words she might possibly need), she locked herself in her room, just as she used to when she had been studying for her exams, and wrote a letter on pink notepaper to someone she had never met.

DEAR MISS PROBLEM-WALLA, c/o EVE'S BEAUTYBASKET, BOMBAY-1: I am a young woman of twenty with wheatish complexion. In addition, I am well versed in Rabindra singing, free-style dancing to Tagore's music, sitar playing, knitting and fancy cooking. I weigh 48 kilos and am considered slim. My hair is jet black, hip-length and agreeably wavy. If you were to say to me that with such endowments I am a fortunate person, you would be almost correct. There is just one annoying flea in my ointment. The flea is my flat chest. As I am sure you realize, this defect will adversely affect my chances of securing an ideal husband and will sorely vex the prowess of even the shrewdest matchmakers in this great nation. Therefore I'm sure you will agree it is imperative that I do something about my problem and enhance my figure to the best of my ability. Please do not, I beg you, advocate chicken soup, homeopathic pills, exercises and massages. I have tried them already. The icing on my cake was drinking two lemons squeezed in warm water first thing in the morning for ten days, with the result that I lost three-quarters of a centimeter from you know where. Need I say that I am desperate, almost suicidal? I see life slamming its doors in my face. I want to live!

I look to you now, dear MISS PROBLEM-WALLA, dear prophet and saviour of us suffering women, to pull a magical remedy from your proverbial beauty basket. Help me! YRS., ETC., HOPELESS BUSTLESS

After she had mailed the letter she wept for three hours. She did not expect her letter to be printed. It was too sincere, too passionate; it exposed too much. She visualized Miss Problem-Walla in her air-conditioned Bombay office, sitting regally on rubbery thighs, with painted nails and legendary breasts. Could such a woman be expected to *feel*, to actually share her anguish?

Dimple's letter was not printed or answered.

On dark September nights in Rash Behari Avenue, when the wooden wardrobe cast odd shadows on the scalloped headboard of her bed, she invented desperate schemes. Cosmetic surgery in the West! Transplant Nearly Human Cones on Offensively Flat Flesh! On such nights, she looked in the bathroom for her father's razor blades. She thought of death.

Mrs. Dasgupta had no sentimental side. She told Dimple not to mope but to stand straight and take deep breaths near the window. Dimple responded sullenly to such advice. She looked down from the window into the backyard, at the blistered backs of other houses, and took shallow breaths of dusty air.

In October her mother said, "A good photo is half the battle."

Dimple protested that she looked dreadful in photographs, morose and heavy-lidded. She retrieved the family album from a dusty suitcase under the bed. There were only two pictures of her, grown, in the entire album. It was as though, after her initial plumpness, her father had lost all interest in photographing her. In one she sat cross-legged on the floor, hugging a sitar to her body. In the other she stood in front of a dry fountain in a friend's garden, looking vengeful. "You see what I mean?" she cried, pointing at a crack in the fountain. She hated the family album, hated all those stiff, tiny, rectangular moments from the past, yellowing in the corners where her father's thumb had glued them decisively to the page.

"Don't be a fool," Mrs. Dasgupta scolded. "A little pancake make-up and strong studio lights will do wonders."

The photographs, as it turned out, were a good investment. She looked quite passable, with hair arranged in soft waves and bell-shaped gold earrings peeking, as if by accident, through the hair. "Remember what I said!" her mother laughed. "I'll get you an outstanding boy. I'll make you a real woman!"

Dimple liked the girl in the photograph; it was a marriageable face. Erotic fantasies began to sneak into her mind. Male faces: cricket stars, young cabinet ministers, heroes from novels. Her heart grew vulnerable and paper-thin, transparent as butterflies' wings. On sunny mornings the sight of boxer shorts hanging out to dry on a neighbor's balcony made her blush. At night she hallucinated. Sometimes when she entered the bathroom in the dark, the toilet seat twitched like a coiled snake. Tight, twisted shapes lunged at her from behind cupboards or tried to wrestle her into bed. These too, her mother said, were part of getting married. Next door the boy with water in his head sang:

> This flute is cracked and broken,
> Why do you ask it to sing again?

Dimple invited Pixie for tea four days a week and listened to film gossip. Her bedroom, shuttered against the light, whispering with the fan, was like a hospital room. People were paying their last respects; with marriage so near they did not expect to see her again. "I *do* believe in short engagements," she confided to Pixie, feeling that she was already the girl in the picture, wise enough to offer an opinion, "no more than two or three weeks. And a honeymoon"—the English

word no longer leaped at her—"at the Grand Hotel."
She took to sewing, made her own *choli* blouses,
scooping the neck and lifting the waist to honeymoon
dimensions. Marriage, she was sure, would free her,
fill her with passion. Discreet and virgin, she waited
for real life to begin.

November passed. Then December. Dimple Dasgupta sat on her bed and read novels; she had given up
the idea of taking university exams. The sense of ur-
gency she had had in the summer vanished after the
rains.

"What do you do all day?" Pixie asked. "Just read
novels? Why don't you take typing lessons like me?"

"I indulge in sexual fantasies," Dimple said.

"What kind?"

"Well, they're never *physical*."

In mid-January, when the weather had turned quite
chilly and Dimple had to use a quilt in bed, Mr. Dasgupta announced that he had found his "ideal boy."
The candidate was:

AMIT KUMAR BASU, 29, consultant engineer with
7 years' experience; son of late Ajoy Kumar Basu
(Outward Bills Department of The Chartered
Bank, Calcutta). Dependents: Widowed mother
and younger brother studying Physics Honours in
Presidency College.

Advantages: 1) Has already applied for immigration to Canada and U.S.; also has job application
pending in Kenya. 2) Older sister married to
Chartered Accountant (P. K. Ghose) with important family connections and might be able to fa-

cilitate process of getting passport, visas, etc. for
bride of candidate.

Mr. Dasgupta had the horoscope checked, made pre-
liminary inquiries about dowry requirements (he said
he was prepared to give the usual gold ornaments, saris,
watch and fountain pen, some furniture, perhaps, but
absolutely not a scooter or a refrigerator) and arranged
an informal tea at his home so the candidate and his
mother and sister could meet Dimple.

Later Dimple told Pixie that she had been too nervous to take a good look but that she thought he was
like the young executives in clothing ads: a lean young
man in a business suit, dazzling white teeth, thin mustache. He had asked her what her hobbies were.

Mr. Dasgupta took a month's leave from work to
complete the negotiations and pull off the wedding.
There were two early hitches: Mrs. Basu objected to
the name Dimple, which she considered too frivolous
and unBengali, and the candidate's sister, Mrs. Ghose,
felt that Dimple was a little darker than the photograph
had suggested. With the Basus, Mr. Dasgupta flattered
and pleaded, smiling at Dimple and saying, "She is so
sweet and docile, I tell you. She will never give a moment's headache." At home, he advised his wife to try
more whitening creams and homemade bleaching
pastes. After two weeks, Mrs. Basu and Mrs. Ghose
conceded it was a satisfactory match. But they had made
their point: Dimple Dasgupta was not their first choice.

The wedding date was fixed for early February. Mr.
Dasgupta planned to hold the actual wedding ceremony
on the roof of his house on Rash Behari Avenue. Everyone hoped no sudden squalls or cold waves would
ruin the outdoor arrangements.

"What a lucky girl you are!" Pixie exclaimed. "You'll be in America before you know it. I'll still be slogging away at my typing and shorthand."

"Who knows? I might find myself in Kenya instead," Dimple said grimly.

She spent two weeks shopping every day, twice a day. She thought of herself as someone going into exile. In those two weeks, she met her fiancé a second time. He and Mr. and Mrs. P. K. Ghose took her to see an old film at the Ramakrishna Mission, then for cold coffee at Kwality's on Gariahat Road. On the way back, Dimple and her fiancé sat by themselves in the back seat of Mr. Ghose's Fiat, with his sister watching them through the rearview mirror. He talked of his hobby: cricket.

There were no squalls or cold waves on the day of the wedding, and only two minor "mishaps," as Mr. Dasgupta called them, occurred. In the morning, Dimple cut her thumb trying to unscrew a new bottle of coconut hair oil and had to have it bandaged. And out of eighty-five kilos of fish delivered by the Dasguptas' regular fishmonger in Lake Market, ten kilos were bad and had to be thrown away. From the window of the bathroom on the wedding morning, Dimple saw crows and pariah dogs work through the rotten fish that had been thrown in an open dump in the alley behind the house.

It was a perfect wedding. There were one hundred and five photographs to prove that it was perfect. Mrs. Dasgupta's youngest brother, who was a photographer for a Bengali newspaper, had taken pictures of the old men chewing betel leaves and spitting red juice on rented mattresses; young women braiding the bride's hair with traditional red ribbons and tinsel; the bride trying to conceal her bandaged finger behind the folds of her red, bridal brocade; children sleeping on sofas;

women on the roof blowing conch shells; and the groom stepping out of a green Fiat decorated with red and white garlands.

Pixie and her friends threw petals at the groom as he got out of his car and walked through the specially illuminated front gate to the living room, which had been reserved for him. They loved the stiff, athletic way he walked, just like a cricket bowler, and the way he brushed the petals off his shoulders, like a movie star at a *mahurat*. He smiled at the photographer and laughed at something Mr. Dasgupta said.

Then they raced back to Dimple's bedroom, where she sat draped in a heavy sari and veiled in gold. She was in agony. "He's arrived, Dimple! So handsome, I cannot tell you. And so serious, so much in control." They had forgotten his nervous smiles, his short, intense laugh over Mr. Dasgupta's memorized joke. They wondered what else Dimple would like to hear.

"Yes," said Pixie, a little carried away, "Amitabh Bachchan the second."

"Your short, dark Prince Charming!"

"So strong! My goodness, you can tell he has personality!"

"But I thought he was tall!" Dimple cried. "I distinctly remember he looked tall when he sat next to me at Kwality's the other day."

The first evening in the Basus' flat on Dr. Sarat Banerjee Road, Dimple sat with her husband on a low, wide bed and listened to him talk about cricket. He had a deep, persuasive voice; she thought of the times years ago when she had seen the boy with water in his head play cricket in the alley behind her house.

When it was time to sleep, Amit said, "Of course,

this is only a temporary arrangement. My immigration should come through any day.''

"You mean *our* immigration."

"Yes. It takes a little time getting used to, you know."

Not for me, she thought. But not to seem disloyal, she meekly agreed.

"Which country do you want? Kenya, Canada or the U.S.?"

"Whichever one you want."

"I'll take whichever one comes through first. A man must be decisive."

"So, now I learn I've married a gambler." She tried to giggle like a newly-wed. Thoughts of living in Africa or North America terrified her. She wanted to know how long they would stay, but she didn't know quite how to ask it without revealing her fear. He made a hesitant attempt to squeeze her waist.

"There's one small thing," he said. "My mother wants to call you Nandini. She doesn't like Dimple as a name."

"What will you call me?"

"Nandini, Dimple . . . what's in a name, for goodness sake?"

"Everything," Dimple said.

By the third week in February, Amit went back to work and Dimple tried to get used to being called Nandini.

"It's not easy," she said to Pixie on the phone. "The name just doesn't suit me." The phone was in the landlord's apartment on the second floor and she had to ask his permission each time she called her mother or Pixie. She was sure he listened in and reported every word to her mother-in-law. "I don't *sound* like a Nandini."

"How does a Nandini sound?"

"How should I know?"

"Oh, you'll get used to it in no time. The main thing is to get your mother-in-law on your side."

"Look who's talking! You're not even married yet."

"But how about other things? Seriously, Dimple, are you okay? Are you happy and all that?"

"Everything's fine," she said, dropping her voice as low as she dared, "except for the apartment. The apartment is h-o-r-r-i-d." She quickly spelled the last word in English.

The apartment was on the top floor of a three-story building on Dr. Sarat Banerjee Road. The entrance was a narrow alley that led off the sidewalk to a warped green door at the side of the building. The electric bell on the frame of the green door had been ripped out and had not been replaced. The staircase was shared by the tenants of the upper two floors; there were no electric outlets in the staircase area so the tenants had to use flashlights in the dark. The front door opened on to the main living area. Beyond the front room were two other rooms, used as bedrooms, then a small courtyard, off which were a bathroom and a kitchen. The living room had a blue Rexin sofa, two wooden office chairs, a low table covered with a cloth, a cabinet with glass doors, and a rack for shoes and sandals, since the Basus did not wear shoes inside the apartment. There were framed batik goddesses on the walls—the handiwork of Mrs. Ghose as a schoolgirl. The cabinet was full of painted clay fruits and china dolls, a house made of match sticks, two sandalwood elephants that had lost their trunks and small, tarnished silver trophies. On the blue Rexin sofa were five hard cushions, on which Mrs. Basu and Mrs. Ghose had embroidered dancing peacocks.

Dimple did not like to sit on that sofa or lean back against the hard cushions.

The first bedroom—it led directly off the living room and was windowless—was used by Mrs. Basu and Amit's younger brother, who was called Pintu at home though his formal name was Ranjit Kumar. There was a narrow bed on which Mrs. Basu sat or slept in the daytime; at night, when Pintu used the bed, separate bedding was unrolled for her on the floor. Old suitcases, wrapped in newspaper to protect them from the dust, were stored on top of the wardrobe. Within a week of her arrival, Dimple's suitcases had also been wrapped and stored above the others.

Dimple's room was exactly the same size as the other bedroom, except that it had two windows. It had a large double bed with a giant swan carved on the headboard, a metal wardrobe for clothes, a dressing table with an oval mirror and a metal desk. The dressing table and wardrobe had come from Mr. Dasgupta: Amit had declined other furniture in lieu of cash settlement, as he expected to leave Calcutta as soon as his immigration came through. Dimple wished she could have at least chosen the curtains in her room. She hated the gray cotton with red roses inside yellow circles that her mother-in-law had hung on sagging tapes against the metal bars of the windows. In the magazines that Pixie had brought her in those days of waiting on Rash Behari Avenue, "young marrieds" were always going to decorators and selecting "their" colors, especially their bedroom colors. That was supposed to be the best part of getting married: being free and expressing yourself.

The courtyard was almost perfectly square and partly roofed. There were five crotons in clay pots in a row in the open area, and almost hidden behind two pots was Amit's homemade slingshot for killing crows.

"Your father did *not* mislead you," Mrs. Dasgupta said on the phone. "He said it was a three-room apartment with a nice courtyard and a row of crotons."

"He didn't tell me about the staircase. There's no light on the staircase."

"Don't they have a torch? Anyway, it's temporary for you."

"I hurt my elbow last night."

"Any word yet on your going abroad?"

"No. He didn't tell me about the water either. The water has to be carried up in buckets and stored. The tap in the bathroom is broken."

"Well, that can . . ."

"He didn't tell me about the water," Dimple repeated, and hung up.

There were other things—Pintu coughing in the bathroom, spiders behind the kitchen door—that she could not even talk about on the telephone.

"Dimple Basu," she said to the oval mirror in the bedroom. "Dimple Basu is an exciting name." There was a sound of coughing in the next room and she was ashamed that she had been talking to herself. She picked up a comb and ran it through her hair so that anyone walking into her room would think she had been combing her hair after a bath. Happy people did not talk to themselves and happy people did not pretend that they had not been talking to themselves. "Dimple Basu," she repeated. "Dimple Basu is a happy woman."

That evening Amit took her to Kwality's by taxi and ordered chili chicken, chicken fried rice and chicken spring rolls, because at home Mrs. Basu permitted only fish. There were three other diners. Amit sat very close to her and held her hand under the table.

"I don't think your sister likes me," Dimple said.

"Let's talk about what we'll do in Toronto or New York," Amit said.

"What's the capital of Kenya?"

"Who cares? I'm keeping my fingers crossed about the other two."

"Why doesn't your sister like me?"

"Who said she doesn't? She likes you."

She heard Amit talking in a strange, furry whisper. He wanted her to call him Mit, or Mitu, and sit even closer—but she could not hear herself speak. She ate large spoonfuls of fried rice and worried about the most discreet way of eating chili chicken. It was difficult to tackle the small pieces with knife and fork, but eating with her fingers, Bengali-style, in a restaurant, seemed terribly uncouth. He should have taken her to Trinca's on Park Street, where she could have listened to a Goan band play American music, to prepare her for the trip to New York or Toronto. Or to the discotheque in the Park Hotel, to teach her to dance and wriggle. Or did he know how? She let her hands stay under the table but they were limp and resentful, she knew.

"We must do this every week," Amit said. "There's no privacy at home."

To please her husband, Dimple took to wearing bright colors: reds, oranges, purples. She wore her hair up in a huge bun and let a long wispy curl dangle behind each ear, like Mrs. Ghose. She even tried to imitate the way Mrs. Ghose laughed and left sentences half-finished. She gave up eating her favorite hot green chilis.

"You look very nice," Amit said. "Very different but very nice." He said such things only very late at night, after dinner was over and the plastic cloth on the table had been wiped clean and the servant had gone downstairs (he slept on the landing close to the warped green door) and Pintu had put away his books and turned off the light in the next room.

"Which one do you like better? The old me or the new one?"

"I like them both. You know I love you."

"But I want you to *say* things to me. The way husbands are supposed to."

"I'm not good at saying things." He had a way of making that sound naughty. She let him grab her and push her down among the pillows and fall on top of her. Sometimes in bed she thought of the baby lizard she had found in her pillowcase. His deep, persuasive voice faded into grunts and gurgles.

When her husband was at work and she was at home helping Mrs. Basu air winter clothes and put them away with mothballs and *neem* leaves in a trunk—the servant cooked and cleaned and did all the heavy work—she told herself it should be easy to love Amit. He was quite handsome, not in the way movie stars were, but in the way real people sometimes were. His face was very symmetrical, with large eyes and a square jaw and high cheekbones. She liked his hair, especially the way it curled in the back, and the little mole just below the hairline on his neck. She did not like his paunch. It was not quite a paunch yet, but if he ate the greasy foods that the Basus seemed to love he would end up with a stomach like a helium-filled balloon. But there was something destructive in trying to recall his features like that, she felt; the sum of the parts did not add up to the whole. Bombay movie stars knew how to pretend they were in love. She tried to speak their *filmi* language when Amit was not at home: "*Arré yaar*, this Mitu is such a yummy lovey-dovey pie, I want to bite a piece of him off." But then she could not imagine him in flashy shirts and imported aviator glasses because he was standing there in front of the oval mirror unknotting his tie. She could only say, "Did you have a good day at the office? Can I bring you your fresh lime and water now?" In those hours that he was away, any face in a magazine was fair game. She borrowed a forehead from an aspirin ad, the lips, eyes and chin from a bodybuilder and shoulders ad, the stomach and legs from a trousers ad and put the ideal man and herself in a restaurant on Park Street or by the side of a pool at a five-star hotel. He wore blue bathing trunks, there was no ugly black hair on his back and shoulder blades as he leaped feet first into the pool while she stood on the edge in a scarlet sari with a gold border, behind wraparound sunglasses, and trailed her toes in the water.

Pintu told Dimple that he was in love with a girl in his class at Presidency College but that he had never talked to her. "I know she is aware of me," he said. "I can tell when a person is aware of me but does not look at me. This girl is aware of me, like that."

"How can you tell?" Dimple asked.

"From the way she doesn't look at me."

"You mustn't laugh," Amit said one night in bed. "I haven't talked about this to anyone." Then he told her about his dream for retirement in a pink house in Kalyani with a vegetable garden in back and a lawn in front and a lily pool with goldfish in the middle of the lawn. "It has to be pink," he said. "I'm adamant about that."

"We could have some statues on the lawn," Dimple said. "I'd like a Venus with arms."

"I'll settle for a pink Venus."

For the rest of the week they took to going to bed earlier and earlier so they could talk of the pink Venus.

* * *

When Pintu announced that he had started giving math lessons to a twelve-year-old boy on Rash Behari Avenue so that he could pay for his own movie tickets and postage stamps for letters to a pen-friend in Japan, Dimple had her first convulsion of regret that she had not taken the university exams. She told Amit, "I bet he has a girl friend and he needs money to take her out."

But Amit laughed at her. "What a hopeless romantic you are. He's only nineteen! What does he know about girls?"

"Who cares about an old woman like me?" Mrs. Basu said one morning from her bed on the floor, under the mosquito netting. "Who cares for anyone these days?"

Dimple crawled in under the net and put her hand on the older woman's forehead. The skin was hot and dry; she thought hot, dry skin was repulsive. She crawled out again and untied the mosquito net from the wall hooks, careful not to let it collapse on Mrs. Basu's body.

"Watch it!" Mrs. Basu exclaimed. "You almost smothered me with that net! You want to kill me so you can get my gold bangles!"

Amit took a thermometer out of the metal wardrobe, washed it with soap and water, then checked his mother's temperature. Mrs. Basu had a temperature of 101 degrees. He showed Dimple how to read the thermometer and told her to check again around twelve-thirty.

"I can't," said Dimple. "I can't tell where the thread of mercury is; it's too fine. I'm too stupid about these mechanical things."

"It must be flu," Amit said. "Call the doctor if you think it's necessary." At twelve-thirty she checked Mrs.

Basu's temperature again. But though she held it up to the light and turned it around slowly several times, she could not read the thermometer. Then she flicked her wrist too violently and the thermometer fell on the floor.

"Shall I call the doctor?" Pintu asked when he saw her wiping up the glass bits with a wet rag. "Be careful that the mercury doesn't touch your gold bangles! It'll turn them white."

"What do you think? You tell me." She felt there were too many people in the apartment on Dr. Sarat Banerjee Road, too many people to make demands on her, driving her crazy. "If we call the doctor, we should try to move her up on the bed, don't you think?"

"No one cares," sighed Mrs. Basu. "I know they're waiting for me to die so they can all go off to a foreign country."

"He won't care about her sleeping on the floor. He's been here many times."

Mrs. Basu did not die. But she had high fever for three days, which left her weak and quarrelsome. Dimple went to Lake Market every day to buy tangerines and oranges and squeezed them by hand for her mother-in-law. She wondered how the older woman would react when she found out that the immigration papers were due any week now.

One morning in early April Amit surprised her in the courtyard and said in English, "I always thought I'd marry a tall girl. You know the kind I mean, one meter sixty-one or sixty-two centimeters, tall and slim. Also convent-educated, fluent in English." Then he hooked his umbrella on his wrist and left for his office in a hurry.

From the balcony she watched him run toward the bus stop. It was amazing that one could be intimate with a person for so many weeks and not realize what kind of a person he had *really* wanted to marry. There was nothing she could do about her height except stand straight and dress wisely. But what excuse could she offer him for her spoken English? When his bus had turned the corner, she stole the *Basic Conversational English* from a mildewed bookcase in the living room. The book exhausted her.

Look, sir, look, the bore is rising on the Hooghly.
We're reconnoitering the man-eater in these Hills.
Who passes yonder? It is the water-carrier, the
unsung hero of the day.

She wondered what it meant, to *unsing*.

Dimple turned to magazines in English, taking them to bed with her during the siesta hour, spending hours each afternoon on letters to the editor. Everyone seemed wiser than she, more aware of the great issues, more in touch.

DEAR ED: Re your untoward stand in your article, "Divorce Delhi-Style." To question the goodness and the utility of marriage because statistics of women suicides is grim is to make a foolish and unjust attack on a long-lasting and noble way of life. Marriage is the song of the road and we should all sing it. Otherwise the virtues of our culture will wither and fall off by the wayside. Are you forgetting the unforgettable Sita of legends? Can you not recall how she walked through fire to please Ram, her kingly husband? Did Sita humiliate him by refusing to stroll through fire in front of his subjects and friends? Let us carry the torch (excusable pun!) of Sita's docility!

Marriage alone teaches the virtues of sacrifice,

responsibility, and patience. If we are ready to admit that our society does not need responsible people, e.g., hydraulics engineers, chemists, doctors and industrialists, then we should all be ready to go and live in jungles. Then if "happiness" is our only goal in marriage as you claim, we should all be "happy as monkeys" and then where would our culture be? Or are you suggesting we should live under the thumb of Mr. Mao Tse-Tung? No, no, dear lady editor; just as the man has certain obligations to society, so the wife has obligations to the husband. Infidelity in the husband should not be matched with philandering on the side of the wife. After all, we are not so depraved as Europeans or our own film stars. Kindly do not deprave your readership further. A cheating wife is not to be understood and sympathized with—she is to be turned out like a leper! Two cheers for marriage. Hip, hip! Mrs. INDIRA RAMKUMAR, Indore

Ed: *What was sauce for Sita may no longer be sauce for us—more than our glorious culture is withering by the wayside, my dear. Or haven't you noticed?*

DEAR LADY EDITOR: I was pleased to read your thought-provoking and intellect-stimulating jeu d'ésprit on "Divorce" and related topics. In answer, may I tell you a story? My service club recently received a plea from a village woman (whose name and village shall remain anonymous in this epistle) in which the woman said she was in utter distress because she had been thrown out of doors and rendered roofless by her husband, deprived of respect and property on account of her infertility. So far, she has managed to keep barren body and soul together by begging and other such humiliating activities. Who knows, this woman could, out of sheer despair, turn to worse things, like real sin. It is my belief that there should be a special club or organization for Abused, Helpless Housewives. Instead of "women's lib" types like you causing unrest and tearing the fabric of our society, you should be mending such rips. KA-MALA GANGREDIWAR, Bombay

Ed: *Abused wives, a category embracing perhaps twenty crore women in this country, need political power—not the tender mercies of comfortable urban clubwomen such as you.*

She could not take her eyes off the letters. She wondered what finally happened to the unnamed village woman. Had she died of hunger? Or had she been kidnapped by bad men and forced to engage in unspeakable activities? Dimple invented a happy ending: the woman's mother had sent for a fertility drug from the West and the woman, in time, had borne sextuplets. She thought it dangerous to learn too much English.

When Amit came back from the office and found her in bed with the letters to the editor, he seemed angry.

"Where's my fresh lime and water?"

"I forgot to make it. I'm sorry; I was busy reading."

"But you *know* I like fresh lime and water when I come back. You *know* this little thing means a lot to me."

She played with the magazine, twisting the corners with her fingers, rolling and unrolling them until the cover girls' faces were wrinkled and ugly. His disapproval was torture; all her life she had been trained to please. He expected her, like Sita, to jump into fire if necessary.

"I can make it now," she said. The room seemed too small; there was fluff on the high ceiling. How could fluff cling to a ceiling? It seemed against gravity.

"It's not the same thing," he said. He took off his Western clothes and pulled on a pair of loose *khadi* pajamas and a thin *kurta*. Then, just as she was about to cry as she remembered the barren woman who had been rendered roofless, remembered too the afternoons in Rash Behari Avenue, the oil massages, vitamin pills, the long agonized waiting, he came around the bed, tossed the magazines away, and kissed her on the chin.

"Who said I want fresh lime?" he said roguishly. "You lock the door, Dimple, and I promise you some very interesting things."

The next evening she stood in the courtyard, where the smell from the bathroom was almost overpowering, and watched Amit aim pebbles at crows with his slingshot.

"What can you see in the dark?" She imagined the pebbles flying into the night, past trees and electric poles, and falling with a gentle *plop* into the Dhakuria Lakes. She hated the lakes, thought of them as death, as calm warm water closing over wasted bodies.

"Did you see that?" Amit cried. "I got a good one that time." This was a new Amit, younger than Pintu, it seemed, his low voice tinny with excitement. This must be the real Amit, the boy who lives with his mother and brother in the third-floor flat on Dr. Sarat Banerjee Road. What does he know of marriage?

A crow lay by the crotons. She did not think a

wounded crow, trying to raise itself on one good wing, then falling back, could be so depressing.

Dimple moved away from the porch and into her own room. With her head down on lace doilies (crocheted by Mrs. Ghose, she supposed) she tried to think not of the bird outside but of how much she hated lace doilies. They were too fussy and caught dust. She wished she were brave enough to throw them out of her room and put in things she really liked, like the velvet monkey Pixie had made for her long ago as a birthday gift. She wished she were back in her own room in Rash Behari Avenue, on a bed cluttered with broken-backed books. But not with a name like Nandini: it was so old-fashioned and unsung. Oh, to have walked through fire! Oh, to have had the courage and the passion to be dramatic! It was this passive resistance, this withholding of niggardly affection from Amit, this burying of one's head among dusty, lace doilies that she found so degrading.

"Bull's eye!" chirped Amit from the courtyard. "My total score is up to two hundred and fifty-three!"

By mid-May she had missed a period. She put it down to the excitement of marriage and returned to eating hot green chilis in the hope that her body would return to its normal cycle. Sometimes, under the cover of her loose sari, she gave vicious squeezes to her stomach as if to force a vile thing out of hiding. By the end of the month she had begun to vomit, not just in the mornings as she thought pregnant women did, but at all hours of the day and night, whenever she thought no one was watching. She would sneak off to the bathroom and crouch in front of the toilet bowl with both elbows on the rim and watch the arc of foul vomit crash against the sides. The vomit fascinated her. It was hers; she was locked in the bathroom expelling brownish liquid from her body. She took pride in the brownish blossoms, in the solid debris of chewed cauliflowers and lentils that sank fast; she grew arrogant and possessive, resenting the flush that carried them away to some sea. In her arrogance, she thrust her fingers deep inside her mouth, once jabbing a squishy organ she supposed was her tonsil, and drew the finger in and out in smooth hard strokes until she collapsed with vomiting. Later, when the spasms subsided, she realized she enjoyed the sensation of vomiting, the tightening in the gut, the wild expulsion from the belly. So she tried to recapture the sensation by gripping the toilet bowl with her knees, her sari pulled up and back well over her thighs, tightening and relaxing the stomach muscles, right forefinger groping against tongue and teeth. But it was hard to recapture that pleasure on the second try. In those days a sour smell clung to her hair and clothes; she found it faintly exciting.

Vomiting was real to her, but pregnancy was not. On long afternoons, while the men were at work or in college and her mother-in-law asleep over her newspaper, she sat on the bed in silence trying hard not to think of the changes in her body. The long, overstuffed bolsters on either side of her hurt her hips. She thought of ways to get rid of . . . whatever it was that blocked her tubes and pipes. Her insides were like a clogged drain. She would pour some cleaning powder down her throat—if the powder was advertised as destroying rotting food, fallen hair, grease, it could surely burn its way through muscle, fiber and tissue? She spent her time cataloguing ways to rid herself of *it*. She had heard that some women used castor oil to ease the delivery. At worst, she could arrange to slip in the bathroom or fall down the staircase or sit on a knitting needle, though that would be too obvious to conceal. When she ran out of ideas, she pressed cold compresses on her eyes and thought bitterly that no one had consulted her before depositing *it* in her body. Or was it her fault? She was probably more fertile than others, and there was that poor village woman rendered roofless because of her infertility. Life was too unjust.

One evening after she and Amit had come home from a Mrinal Sen movie and she was about to take two aspirins, because she always got headaches after going to the movies, he said, "Oh no, you don't. I know the big secret. From now on no more aspirins or pills. It's bad for the baby."

Dimple was astonished. She quickly put the aspirins back in their bottle, then took them out again, held them in the open palm of her hand as if they were pearls, perfectly symmetrical, exquisite.

"My head hurts," she said, when she had meant to say, how did you know, have you been listening for noises outside the bathroom door, does my hair smell or perhaps the tips of my fingers?

"Mother told me the secret. Now you've got to take it easy."

In spite of the hot night outside the window, she felt damp and chilly. Even the light bulb fixed at an angle to the wall, the transparent light bulb with its single bright filament, sent a chill through her body. "How about the loop?" she asked. "Why didn't you tell me to get the loop? Why didn't you arrange it?" She visualized the loop like the bright thin coil inside the light bulb.

"Loops are for villagers and poor people," he said.

"We could have tried the pill," she cried. "Why didn't you get me some pills?" Her helplessness enraged her. She needed his informal approval and his know-how for everything. If she ever had to send a cable overseas or send a money order, she would not know how to do it.

"That's for other people," he smiled. "The world deserves our baby."

He took the aspirins out of her hand and threw them out of the window. His gestures were always quick, decisive. She wondered if he ever regretted a word he had said, if he ever suffered nightmares or wished he could turn back time. What a strong face he had; everything about him was solid. He was like a god, with excellent managerial capacities.

"What do I do about my headache now?" she asked. He shrugged his shoulders for a moment, and just as she was about to burst into tears, accuse him of indifference, tell him she hated tyrannical fetuses, he strode across the room to her, put his large, solid hands on her forehead and kneaded her soft, light flesh until the veins stopped throbbing.

"It'll be a boy," Amit said. "He'll be a doctor and mint money."

"Only businessmen make money. Bengalis make bad businessmen," Dimple said. But she knew that there was nothing fraudulent about the Basu family's joy. They looked on the unborn son as communal property and were very solicitous of her health. They laid down rules: do not carry heavy pails of water to the bathroom or the kitchen; do not trip on dark staircases.

But she hated all the Basus; her body swelled violently with unvented hate. In her daydreams, neurosurgeons gave way to sinister abortionists, men with broken teeth and dirty fingers, who dug into her body in a dark, suburban garage. She was obsessed by those imaginary men. Their features were borrowed from men she knew, from the faces of strangers she saw below her as she sat on the balcony. There were games she played with these strangers: she threw bits of newspapers, hair balls, nail clippings, down onto the heads below to make them jerk upward in anger. From those trapped, angry faces she borrowed noses, warts, eyebrows, to be assembled in fantasy in endless combinations of dread. Sleeping was worse than staying awake, for then she was sucked into the center of cone-shaped emotions that made her sweat, cry loudly, sit up in bed. As she got better at these games, she concentrated on her husband's face rather than on strangers'. She picked quarrels with him so she could see his eyes grow dull and sullen and his cheeks sag briefly with hate. She made fun of his dress, spilled curry on his shirtfront at breakfast when she knew it was too late for him to change. If he brought her a gift, a movie magazine or a new historical novel, she laughed and told him he had hopeless taste. But she was not unhappy. Later she thought of it as a brief period of passion, when she had broken through her fortress of politeness. She was glad it had happened.

One morning when she was sitting on the floor of the balcony and picking dead bugs and stone chips out of rice that was to be cooked later in the day, she heard soft, scurrying noises behind her. It could come only from mice, she knew, the mice who were her allies as they worked their way through her pile of paperback romances. But today she hated the invisible mice for disrupting her daydreams—she could not dare borrow features from a rodent!—and she pushed aside the platter of rice, listening for soft scratchy sounds so she could smash life out of the little gray heads. When the noises came again, this time from behind the peeling wooden doors leading to the bedroom, she stood up nervously and grabbed a broom as a weapon. In her hurry to snatch the broom, she stepped on the stainless steel

platter of rice grains. The little toe on her left foot began to bleed. There was a tiny drop of blood, *her* blood,
she thought, astonished, on the coarse, reddish white
grains of rice. It was an added reason for killing the
mouse. She chased it behind the door, thought she saw
a gray furry face dashing into her room, and brought
her broom down again and again on the cement floor.
The noise was in her bedroom now, quick scuffling
strokes among baby clothes that Mrs. Ghose had sewn
and stacked in a wicker basket. She tightened her grip
on the broom and hit the pile of small smocks, so thin
and fine and prettily embroidered; she pounded and
pounded the baby clothes until a tiny gray creature ran
out of the pile, leaving a faint trickle of blood on the
linen. She chased it to the bathroom. She shut the door
so it would not escape from her this time. She hit the
toilet seat viciously with her broom, then the water
drums and the plastic hose.

"I'll get you!" she screamed. "There's no way out
of this, my friend!" She seemed confident now, a
woman transformed. And in an outburst of hatred, her
body shuddering, her wrist taut with fury, she smashed
the top of a small gray head.

It lay behind a plastic pail. Just the head was visible. Horribly misshapen, bloody from the blows. Now
that her passion had subsided and she was almost
calm, she held the broom like a walking stick, and
gently, very gently, eased the broom behind the pail,
pushed out two bobby pins, and finally the rodent
body covered with hair balls, wet, black and matted.
It had a strangely swollen body. A very small creature
with a fat belly. To Dimple the dead mouse looked
pregnant.

* * *

"Are you sure you'll remember?" Pixie asked on the phone. "Eleven-thirty at the Skyroom. I'll tell you all about my new job when we meet."

"See you on Tuesday then." And, defiantly loud: "Eleven-thirty at the Skyroom."

The landlord shifted position in his wicker chair and said, "Skyroom? Skyroom? That's on Park Street!" then returned to the *Ananda Bazar Patrika* he had been reading. She walked out of the room very slowly so that the landlord would not suspect that she disliked him and did not want to talk to him about working-girl lunches and the reputation of Park Street.

On Tuesday morning Pintu took her up to the door of the Skyroom on his way to Presidency College, though it meant he had to go out of his way. They took a minibus, then walked part of the way. On the minibus he showed her a letter he had written:

Dear La Belle Dame Sans Merci: It is a year since I have been in love with you but you do not acknowledge my presence, you never look at me in class, you act moody. How am I to know your mind if you do not give me a hint?

"I'm not going to send the letter to her," Pintu said. "I didn't write it to send; I just wrote it, if you know what I mean."

"Of course," agreed Dimple. She wondered what she would have done if she had received a note like that in class.

"Do you think she's in love with me? I mean, she's going out of her way to ignore me."

"What else can it be?" said Dimple, which seemed to satisfy him. "I'll tell Pixie to drop me off when we are through. So don't worry about the taxi driver running off with me."

Dimple entered the Skyroom, eyes darting from table to table where flashily dressed women sipped iced coffee and held cigarettes aloft, then barricaded herself behind a big table with Pixie.

"I was afraid you'd be late," Dimple said.

"Oh, no. I'm a working girl now. That means I know the golden rule of punctuality."

"I would have died if you were late! I feel terrible when everyone stares at me and I have no one to giggle with."

Pixie sat on the edge of her seat, as if she might have to leave any minute, and swirled the creamy foam in her glass with a drinking straw. In her purple nylon georgette sari and pink plastic beads, she looked like a girl in an ad. Her hair (she said she'd had it cut by a talkative Chinese girl at Eve's on Lindsay Street, then launched into an imitation of Chinese-Anglo-Indian that had Dimple giggling for the first time in nearly six months) was short and shiny, and even her skin seemed to glow and become transparent as if bright lights were trained on her cheeks. To Dimple, she seemed a woman from a bright, inaccessible world. She'd been taken on as a part-time announcer for All-India Radio. She worked in sound booths in the day, and attended cocktail parties ("They think I'm such a character when I only have Cokes") nearly every night. She was following the top woman interviewer around, out to the airport VIP lounge, to the openings of films and plays, to charity banquets. Someday soon ("when they find some VIP who's small enough") they'd promised her an interview of her own. Dimple felt she was on a balcony overlooking that world, and that if anyone gave her a shove she would topple over and disappear in it.

"Tell me everything," she cried to Pixie. "It must be exciting to work in the Akashvani Building!"

Pixie was stingy with the kinds of details Dimple

wanted. She described the cafeteria, the staircase, the little booth her boss sat in; Pixie did not have an office herself. She also said there was a fantastic Steinway. Dimple thought it must be exciting to have a boss, to speak of him so possessively.

"I don't mean describe the pianos in the building, darn it! Tell me the important things." She thought how wonderful to be an announcer, even a part-time one, and wear blackish nail polish and lipstick and talk to a million people in the city.

"What do you mean, the important things?" asked Pixie. "I've told you everything." Dimple watched her scoop delicate peaks of whipped cream from her tall glass and slip them into her mouth. They disappeared between those blackish red lips. She stared at Pixie's shimmering georgette sari, the color of a pigeon's neck in the dim restaurant light, at her satin bright hair. She thought how perfect life would be if she could have a job like Pixie's, and a telephone in her office, and hair styled at Eve's, a boss to frown at her through the glass.

"I don't have a telephone," Pixie said. "I told you, I don't even have my own desk. And some mornings I have to get up at six."

"That's not what I meant," said Dimple.

"What then?"

"I don't know." But she didn't want to let go of Pixie. The subdued laughter of wealthy women frightened her. She didn't belong in the Skyroom. "Can you come for tea tomorrow? I'll make special peas *paratha* for you. I've learned so many new things, you wouldn't believe it!" She thought she heard the strain in her voice.

"Not tomorrow. It's a bad day. Ladies' Study Group tomorrow; big birth control specialist from Germany."

But Pixie promised to come the day after and stay for an hour and a half between work and a party.

When she came for tea two days later she brought a little gift: a goldfish in a glass bowl. She sat on the Rexin sofa in a pink georgette sari and gossiped about her colleagues.

"How's Prince Charming?" she asked.

"He's fine."

"Still charming?"

"Of course. More charming every day."

"You're lucky. I wish I could find a prince!"

Dimple trailed a fingertip in the goldfish bowl and listened to Pixie gossip about her colleagues. Pixie was a figure in her dream: she thought if she stopped listening to Pixie's voice, Pixie would vanish.

That night before she fell asleep, she said to Amit, "When I was a little girl I pulled a snake by its tail. I pulled it straight out of its hole! Can you believe that?"

"There aren't any snakes in the city."

"It was in Bihar. My grandfather was the manager of a colliery or something. I was two and a half and I was very brave."

"Shall I tell you about the time I wrestled with a python? Or the time I fought a tiger?"

He did not believe that she had pulled the snake. She had no memory of the incident, but she knew she had done it because she had heard the story many times from her parents.

"It's true," she said. "You don't have to believe me, but it's true."

"Go to sleep," Amit said, and set an example by turning on his stomach so she could not see the dark lines of his face. The goldfish, swimming mightily, had withstood three flushes of the toilet.

* * *

Dimple and Mrs. Basu came home from Lake Market (the price of fish had gone up again!) and found Amit lying on the sofa with an icebag on his head.

"You're sick!" Mrs. Basu cried. "You're dying!"

"No, I'm not sick. I've resigned from work, that's all."

He stayed on the sofa all day, though he was persuaded to give up the icebag lest he get a cold, drank a record twenty-three cups of tea and muttered, "It was a matter of principle. I refused to budget for a bribe." After dinner he moved into the bedroom and turned it into a fortress: the windows were shuttered, the desk cleared and brought close to the bed so he could use the bed as his desk and write applications and letters. Dimple brought him paper clips, note paper, newspaper ads and fresh cups of tea on the half-hour. Once she brought him a parrot in a rusty cage from a vender on the road, and saw his bitterness soften.

"You shouldn't waste money," he said.

Pintu, whose exams were being postponed, bravely offered to go to work. Dimple, with no degree and not a single marketable skill, offered to go back home. Mrs. Basu waited for the onset of a final disease. Only Amit seemed confident of his abilities. "I have contacts; I have a reputation. They know I am honest."

"It's temporary," Dimple said hopefully. "The immigration papers will come through very soon." She had not thought of Canada or America as real countries until now, only names that people dropped in conversation whenever they could ("My cousin is coming from Calgary for five weeks' vacation and we want to get him married to a nice girl").

"Do you really want to go? Are you sure?" she asked, not knowing which answer she feared more.

"I would go tomorrow."

In the next two weeks he bought nine more parrots from the same vender. Every morning after breakfast he took the parrots one by one out of their cages, stroked their soft, green heads, let them hop on the bedspread and leave droppings on the application forms and books.

Dimple threatened to sleep on the floor.

She tried to crochet a cap for the baby, then gave it up. For two hours she dusted and wet-ragged the floors. This meant moving trunks out from under the beds and dragging the sofa. Sometimes she scared roaches out of dark corners. If the roach was slow, she hit it with her broom until the hard shell broke and the whitish liquid splattered. She was sure there were no roaches in America. The muscles in her back ached; the pain spread to her thighs and calves. There was a strange tightening in the lower part of her stomach. She knew she ought to rest, put her feet up on the arms of the sofa, settle a hard cushion against the small of the back where the pain was furious. She worked harder, running up and down the three flights with plastic pails of water.

"I want everything to be nice and new," Dimple whispered on the phone to Pixie. "I'm not taking any of my old saris when we go to America or Canada."

"You'll be too busy with the baby to go shopping. Keep some of your old ones."

"No. Everything has to be brand-new. That's essential."

"But you haven't heard anything on your immigration yet, have you? What if it doesn't come through?"

She couldn't tell Pixie anything about Amit's job-hunting, the tension, for fear the landlord would evict them. "It has to come through. They can't do that to us. It would be too terribly unfair!" When she hung up she had a vision of her baby. It had wrinkled skin like a very old man's and a large head filled with water.

She began to think of the baby as unfinished business. It cluttered up the preparation for going abroad. She did not want to carry any relics from her old life; given another chance she could be a more exciting person, take evening classes perhaps, become a librarian. She had heard that many Indian wives in the States became librarians.

"It's not like murder," Dimple said one afternoon in June. "I could never commit murder!" If she had planned it for months, she would have used something flashy—a red hot poker from the kitchen or large sewing scissors—but if she had planned it, she knew, her anger would have chilled to inaction. She would have become discreet and adaptable as usual. Certainly she would not have picked a skipping rope as her weapon. Who would have thought you could skip your way to abortion? Dimple was as surprised as the others.

It was difficult to reconstruct the exact details. She remembered the bathroom floor was slippery, especially near the mouth of the large drain. And there was a smell; it was everywhere, on the shelves lined with newspaper, on the toothbrushes and soap dishes and pumice stones and loofas; even the towels hanging from a nail behind the door smelled bad. She had skipped rope until her legs grew numb and her stomach burned; then she had poured water from the heavy bucket over her head, shoulders, over the tight little curve of her stomach. She had poured until the last of the blood washed off her legs; then she had collapsed. It was Pintu who had carried her to bed and summoned the doctor.

No one noticed the skipping rope, coiled under the plastic pail.

"How could it happen to us?" Amit cried. "It was going to be a boy! I was going to teach him cricket! This must be a bad omen!"

"He would have been deformed," Dimple whispered. "I had this bad dream last week . . . he had no arms and legs. I didn't want to tell you; I didn't want to tell anyone so it wouldn't happen."

In the hospital, a nurse called Philomina Thomas showed her a tattered copy of *McCall's Pattern Fashions*, while Dimple tried to rest. She had lost a lot of blood. Philomina Thomas said that her sister had sent her the magazine from Moose Jaw, Canada. It snowed all the time in Moose Jaw, Canada, and Philomina's sister wore galoshes ten months of the year. Dimple prayed that America would answer quickly.

And miraculously, they did. While she was still in the hospital, Amit finally heard that they could immigrate to the United States. She had been looking at a row of little girls in seersucker skirts perched on chrome stools in a soda fountain in Philomina Thomas's magazine, when Amit came rushing into the room with his news. She had never seen him so excited. He hugged and kissed her like a movie star husband. She heard the nurse giggle from the corner chair where she'd been eating tangerines and spitting seeds expertly at passing pedestrians on the other side of the window grille. Amit told her he had let the parrots go. She agreed it would be impossible to take them to the States.

"I know I won't live much longer," Mrs. Basu said when she saw Amit go out to mail a letter to a friend in New York. "I'll die before you come back. Who

cares about an old woman? You go and have a good
time in New York.'' She did, in truth, look ghastly. She
lay in bed all day staring at the ceiling fan. Dimple had
to force her to eat so she would not fall ill and complicate Amit's plans. ''Forty-nine years old, almost fifty,
and alone with just a boy and servant! Who cares about
old people these days?''

In the weeks before leaving, Amit was very tense.
He wrote to three friends in New York and New Jersey,
though he had already heard from his old friend, Jyoti
Sen—they had been roommates at the Institute of Tech-
nology in Kharagpur—offering to put them up in his
Queens apartment until Amit found a job. Dimple
thought it was like living with a new person: she had
to learn to please him in new ways.

Every morning he dressed very carefully in starched
shirts, new bright ties and his suit pants and left the
house with a zippered plastic case full of travel documents. She did not know where he went or what he did
precisely, but she knew it had something to do with
satisfying the Americans, the Indians, the travel agent
and old Calcutta friends demanding favors. She assumed he was standing in long queues in musty office
buildings, collecting more documents, since he seemed
to bring home more forms than he left with. She was
happy to leave the real work to him, while she herself
took care of frivolous details. During the day she took
winter clothes out of the trunk (there was a hand-knitted
cardigan, two sweaters and a Balaclava cap the late Mr.
Basu had worn on a trip to Darjeeling); she spent the
evenings mending bugholes. She sewed long-sleeved
blouses for herself and bought a dozen cotton petticoats
from a hawker near Gariahat Market. In the early afternoons, instead of sleeping or reading novels as she
had done when she was pregnant, she cleaned out empty

Horlick's bottles and filled them with spices to take with her to the States.

"Don't forget to pack two or three good combs and a packet of big hairpins. Also coconut hair oil," Mrs. Dasgupta said on the phone. "Americans have rotten hair. They don't know anything about hair oils." Dimple obediently went to the store and bought five combs, two packages of sturdy, black hairpins and three bottles of coconut oil, then wrapped them in a cotton petticoat and put them at the bottom of her suitcase. She packed and unpacked her suitcase several times. Leaving Calcutta for good was still unreal to her; sometimes she wanted to take everything she owned, even the velvet monkey Pixie had given her. At other times she wanted to walk onto the plane carrying just a small purse and nothing else.

The day before Dimple and Amit were to leave, Pixie called up and invited them for tea. "Bring Pintu also," she said. "I hear he's a working man these days."

Dimple had expected it to be a small gathering, but it turned out that Pixie had invited eleven other people, mainly announcers and actors. There seemed to be several elegantly bald men, and women wearing imported sunglasses indoors. They talked about famous Bengali filmmakers very familiarly, as if they went to tea with them every week; there was a lot of talk about schedules. Dimple sat in a corner trying not to look frightened. Across the room she heard Amit's deep voice discussing job opportunities in the States with one of the bald men who had just returned.

"You're so lucky!" Pixie said to Dimple in the sexy voice she had cultivated since she started broadcasting. "I wish *I* were leaving tomorrow!" She bit into a pretty chutney sandwich and smiled at someone behind Dimple's head. "Come and meet my friend Dimple Basu. She's leaving for the States tomorrow! Isn't she lucky?"

She turned and faced an older woman, who smiled tolerantly at them both. Hers was an authoritative tolerance, the kind that made people defer to her but behind her back call her catty. "My name is Ratna Das," she said. She had the slow, clear enunciation as well as the flashy make-up of an actress. She said her name with the clear expectation of wonder or surprise from whoever heard it.

"I still haven't finished packing," Dimple giggled. She wished she could think of witty, inconsequential things to say at parties. And it was not true that she had not finished packing; except for her toothbrush, passport and gold jewelry, her suitcase was packed and ready to be carried out into a taxi.

"It might be fun to go for a vacation," Ratna Das said. Dimple thought she had picked up the mannerisms of the actresses and probably went to all the *filmi* parties, but was a little too fleshy to be an actress herself. "But I wouldn't want to settle there." She crinkled her nose in a way that commanded agreement.

"Me too," Pixie said. "I wouldn't want to feel a foreigner all my life. I'm sure it would ruin my *system*." She laughed, doubling up daintily until her shiny hair fell all over her face.

"But why would you feel like a foreigner if you went as an immigrant?"

"*You* may think of it as immigration, my dear," said Ratna Das in her deepest voice, "but what you are is a *resident alien*." She smiled, but the words sounded venomous. Without bothering to excuse herself, Ratna Das drifted away to the other side of the room where a semicircle of middle-aged men with sideburns that flared gray and covered their ears welcomed her with open arms. "What I was saying," a heavy man repeated very loudly, "was that the trouble with the industry today is the abominable quality of film scripts. Unless you produce it yourself, you might just as well forget it. And Ratna—you can quote me!" In the general laughter, Dimple could hear Ratna's voice rising above it. "You know I will, darling." Pixie pointed to a short, bald man in an ascot drinking whiskey by himself in a corner, and whispered to Dimple, "Can you believe *that* nincompoop is Ratna's husband. How could her parents have picked him!"

Dimple thought that Ratna Das would not walk through fire for anybody. Ratna Das was modern and intelligent; perhaps you could not be modern and intelligent and still be heroic. You had to choose between being Sita of the rounded hips who could saunter through fire or being Ratna Das who was, at that very moment, smiling tolerantly at the heavy man and patting his hairless cheeks.

Everyone in the room was laughing and smiling; Dimple had never seen so many people in Calcutta so happy. Older people had always been like her parents; sipping tea and calling each other "Mr." and "Mrs."; real happiness was just in the movies or in the West. She felt a sudden panic that, just as she was being introduced to happy people, she was being taken away again to become a resident alien. The people at Pixie's tea acted as though they were living the happiest lives in the world. When Dimple and Amit said good-bye to Pixie at the front door, Pixie hugged Dimple and wept.

That night in bed, Amit asked her what she was thinking on her last night in Calcutta. He wasn't prepared for her question in return. "It won't be forever, will it?" she asked.

Part Two

J YOTI Sen met them at Kennedy airport and the first question he asked was, "Did you have trouble with customs?" Dimple started to tell of the Horlick's bottles being opened and sniffed, but Amit shushed her: everything was fine; no trouble. Jyoti was fatter and taller than Dimple had expected—she wouldn't have taken him for a Bengali at first sight. His hair was long and his sideburns were even longer; she'd never seen so much hair on an Indian, from so close. Dimple thought he was not on good terms with his new long hair. "You can tell an Indian who lives here by his double chin," Jyoti laughed. "And you can tell one who's just arrived by all that greasy kid stuff." Jyoti wore a red shirt and bright white pants, something a Bombay film star might try to wear. She couldn't believe he was an engineer.

He spoke in a fast and funny mixture of English and Bengali, and Dimple wondered if in a few months she and Amit too would speak that curious language. He kept pointing out buildings, roads, names of suburbs,

51

insulting other drivers while keeping his window rolled up. He was full of news about a triple murder in Queens, something he'd heard on the car radio on the way to the airport. "Jesus Christ, man, in a soda fountain!" he said. "Can you beat that? Some guy came in and asked for a chocolate ice-cream cone and the guy said he only had vanilla and strawberry, so he took out a gun and shot him and two other customers! Christ, nothing's sacred anymore. I tell Meena not to go out unless she absolutely has to."

She wanted to learn more about the triple murder. Jyoti wanted to tell them what every factory along the highway made and how well it was doing. Amit wanted to know only what kind of job he might expect to get. He asked questions on starting salaries, rents for apartments in Queens where the Sens lived, food costs and gasoline shortages. Dimple sat in the back seat of the Cutlass—it was so big and fancy she could stretch out in it as if it were a bed and fall asleep; Calcutta Ambassadors and Fiats had seats like those in airplanes. To keep awake she concentrated on the skyscrapers, taller than anything in Calcutta, and on the enormous cars speeding in regimented lanes. She had never seen such bigness before; the bigness was thrilling and a little scary as well. She couldn't imagine the kind of people who had conceived it and who controlled it. They were going so fast and so quietly, with no obstructions and no horns blowing ("Here," said Jyoti, "if you honk your horn at some guy, he's likely to blow your head off") that she couldn't read the green signs overhead. Jyoti kept changing lanes until they were finally off the superhighway and onto a wide, traffic-clogged boulevard.

"Wait'll you see the skyscrapers, man. We'll go to a party tomorrow night in Manhattan. This stuff here is

just apartment buildings. Christ, you know, I've been
in that soda fountain. If I'd gone there this morning,
who knows, you might still be waiting at Kennedy.''

Meena Sen opened the front door to the apartment
before Jyoti rang the bell. ''I could hear Bengali in the
hall,'' she laughed. She was a large, plain woman with
a flat near-Nepali face, who seemed about ten months
pregnant. A very small girl in a brown dress hung
around her legs, pulling a very loud, squawking toy.
Through the open door behind Meena Sen's head was
a framed batik wall hanging: King Ram and his court
in splendid array, and off to the left, in the background,
fighting for attention with trees, mountains, monkeys
and holy men, a small bonfire and a short, voluptuous
Sita hip-deep in pale orange flames. Cluttering the hall
were a stroller and three more loud, bright pull-toys.
Jyoti and Amit carried the bags into the bedroom. Dimple stood in the hallway, afraid to move with such a
little child underfoot.

''You must be so tired after your trip! Tea will be
ready in five minutes. Real Darjeeling tea. I reserve it
for special friends.''

''The best Darjeeling teas are exported,'' Amit
laughed. ''We have to come to New York to have good
Indian tea. What a joke!''

The little girl, whose name was Archana, would not
let go of her mother's sari. Dimple offered her a candy
and a towelette she had been given on the plane, but
the little girl would not go to Dimple and sit next to
her on the sofa. ''Archana is very shy,'' Meena Sen
said. On the whole, Dimple was glad.

They sat in the living room and had tea and coffee
cake. The women sat on the sofa and, since there were
no other chairs in the room, the men sat on the rug by

the coffee table. Dimple thought the rug was very pretty; it was wall-to-wall, yellow with little blue specks. It was the first wall-to-wall carpet she'd ever seen. There were other pretty things in the room: a television on a fancy stand with a rack for magazines, a tea trolley that could be plugged into the wall to keep food warm, a stereo set with large speakers at the far corners of the room, a two-shelf bookcase that held a transistor radio, a cassette tape recorder, a plastic floral arrangement and eight engineering books. Dimple had never seen television; she prayed that someone would turn it on.

"The floor must be uncomfortable for you," Meena Sen apologized.

"Who needs chairs!" Amit cried. "This is just like home."

"But don't the *sahebs* complain?" Dimple asked.

"Only one way to keep a *saheb* from complaining," Jyoti eagerly explained, "and that's the way we do it: never invite one over." When they saw that Dimple was just smiling, Meena Sen said, "What he means is that they eat nothing but beef—how could I ever go home if I allowed beef in my house? Anyway, who needs *sahebs*? There must be a thousand Indians in just this neighborhood!"

"Meena wants to make a big deal out of it," said Jyoti, still laughing, "when actually she doesn't trust her English for a whole evening. Isn't that right?"

"They're always joking back and forth. They're never sincere. And when they talk to you, you never know when they're serious—*baapré*, I get a headache trying to understand them half the time." The admission of inadequacy chilled the air. "Anyway," Jyoti said, slapping Amit on the back, "with old friends why put on an act? Who wants to buy tons of furniture? You'll only lose money on it when you go back home. I'm going to retire when I'm forty, go back and build a five-*lakh* house and become the maharaja of Lower Circular Road!''

"It used to be thirty-five before," laughed his wife. "Now he's pushed it up to forty."

"If it weren't for the money, I'd go back tomorrow," said Jyoti. "This is too much the rat race for a man like me."

"So long as I don't die here," said his wife.

Dimple asked where they'd gotten the lovely furniture. All second-hand from a Punjabi family who had lived in the next block, Jyoti explained. The Punjabi had advertised on a slip of paper in the shop that sold Indian spices. The family had gone back to Chandigarh.

The coffee cake was delicious. Dimple could not believe it had come out of a box and that all Mrs. Sen had done was add eggs and water, beat it and bake it. Meena took her to the kitchen and showed her a row of prettily packaged cake mixes and puddings. She could visualize herself hostessing a party as Pixie had, and serving cakes and puddings in delicate glass bowls, topped with whipped cream, just like the pictures on the boxes. She could see herself making witty retorts to Ratna Das.

When they returned from the kitchen the men were talking of work.

"I'd say give yourself two months. Things are rather tight just now and the Indian engineer is an expendable guy. On the other hand, they might offer you something no one else will touch. It would be a mistake for you to take it, too. Don't look at anything under seventeen thousand. Living intelligently, you should be able to save at least six thousand a year—and *that's* fifty thousand *rupees*, man." Jyoti was a chemical engineer, a little more highly paid than a mechanical engineer, he explained (Dimple had never understood the distinction between the various kinds of engineers; they all spoke incomprehensible languages—cellulose acetate, poly-acrylonitrile, polyesters and vinyls—magic words with the rhythm of a Sanskrit chant); he earned nearly twenty-five thousand a year, saved ten thousand a year and already had forty thousand dollars in the bank. That wasn't bad, he explained, for someone who'd been over for only five years, although the Gujaratis and some South Indians did even better. He would have done better last year if they hadn't had the baby. A baby could cost you over a thousand dollars. Jyoti got carried away when he talked of earning and saving. Dimple made some simple calculations. Jyoti Sen, at this moment, translated into *rupees*, was worth nearly four *lakhs*. Four hundred thousand, in the language of America. No wonder he looked like a Bombay film star.

"But I can't live off you for two months," Amit objected. "I'll take the first thing and transfer when I have a chance. They will find out soon enough how honest I am." He told the story of his last Calcutta job. Jyoti congratulated him but told him it wouldn't help in New York. Here, you couldn't afford to sound like a trouble-maker, especially if you were an Indian. Work twice as hard, keep your mouth shut, and you'll be a millionaire in fifteen years. Jyoti was talking like a big brother, and it made Amit seem like a child. "Stay with us till you get a good job. You can't afford a mistake right off the bat. Anyway, Meena's going to need help around the apartment; she gets lonely during the day." The living-room sofa pulled out to a double bed.

The women cleared away the tea things and the men went out to get mixes for drinks ("real nonimported

imported Scotch!'') later in the evening. Dimple was happier than she had been for a long time. She thought she was happier now, at that very moment, with a kitchen towel in her hand and a dripping teacup in the other while Meena Sen thrust her hands into soap bubbles in the sink, than she had ever been, even on Rash Behari Avenue.

Dimple stood with her back against the kitchen sink and watched Amit put sugar in his tea. He held the spoonful high over his mug and let the sugar dribble into it. The sugar was beautiful: very fine, very white, without stone chips or ants. She thought she had never really looked at sugar before; it had just been there, gray and gritty and in short supply.

"This is my fifth cup," Amit said. "God knows what it's doing to my stomach. I've got to stop it."

"Don't worry about a job yet," Dimple whispered. "We haven't been here thirty-six hours and you're worrying." She stayed a long time by the sink slicing eggplants; then she soaked them in salted water. "Why do you worry when you are so qualified? Engineers can get jobs in any country."

Three hours later they ran out of tea bags and the two women had to go to the corner store. They put Archana in the stroller and wheeled her around the narrow aisles of the store. Mrs. Sen pointed to cans of pineapple and boxes of cereal, and Dimple did most of the stooping and stretching. Dimple acted very obvious with the cans and boxes in case people might think she was stealing. She put more food in the cart in twenty minutes than she and Mrs. Basu had been able to carry home from Lake Market in two hours.

"Food is very expensive here," Meena Sen said as a bald man in an apron rang up the milk, ice cream, vegetables, cereals, cans of fruit and cleaning fluids. "See that? We came out for tea and I ended up spending ten dollars. Jyoti will be furious."

"I'm sorry," said Dimple.

"Don't be silly," said Meena. "I'm sometimes just a foolish shopper. I'll tell Jyoti it's because of the baby coming and that will be the end of it. Anyway, the way they put things in the store you practically have to buy more than you want. When you start your shopping, Dimple, you'll have to be very careful."

On the way home, still guilty over the costs, Dimple suddenly thought of the perfect solution. And it seemed to her a very *American* thing to do. "Let us buy something for tonight's dessert!" she said to Meena. "What was that thing you served last night?"

"Cheesecake."

"Amit loved it. Let me buy some now!"

Meena agreed to it as a kind of test. Dimple would have to learn to shop soon enough. They were walking slowly behind a fat man with a poodle. The fat man tied his dog to a lamppost and went inside Schwartz's Deli. Meena said, "I'd better stay outside with Archana and the groceries." She picked the girl out of the stroller and put the bag of groceries in the seat. "You go in. Just ask for cheesecake and they'll know what you mean."

Dimple panicked on the sidewalk. She wished she had not mentioned anything about buying dessert. If she had known she would have to go into the store by herself and tell the salesman in English what she wanted and count out the change, she would have kept quiet. "Are you sure, Meena?" she asked. And when Meena said, "Yes, of course," she walked in very quickly, her body taut with fear, walked past the glass case filled with pickles, salads, hanging salamis, nightmarishly

pink roast beef, roast duck and turkey, square slabs of
beige paté, rehearsing her sentence, and finally when
the fat man had stopped laughing over a joke the shop
man had told him, she asked, "Excuse me, please. I
wish to purchase five hundred grams of cheesecake. Do
you have it?"

The air stank of beef blood.

The shop man and the fat man seemed to be staring
at her. She felt her ears go hot and red and she wished
she had insisted on staying outside while Meena went
into the store. Pregnant ladies had more authority. Then
she remembered: *of course*. "I mean one *pound* of
cheesecake," she said. "I'm sorry."

It didn't help. The shop man still stared. "You think
I don't know grams, lady?" She bit her lip. "Grams,
pounds, you think I care? What I care about, lady, is
breaking the law. Tell me—you want I should break the
law?"

"No—I didn't know the law," she said. He was
reaching under the counter, for a gun, Dimple thought.
I've insulted him; I will stand here numbly and be
shot. She couldn't even scream. "Not Abe Beame's
law, lady. Not even the President's law—"

"—that *chazer*," said the fat man.

"*My* law. God's law." He presented a blood-smudged
sign in a language she'd never seen. "If I wanted to
break God's law, I'd sell you cheesecake. But you see
that sign in the window, right under 'Schwartz's'? Look
at it good, lady, and don't ever come into a shop like it
and ask for cheesecake." His face was red, and the
blood-smudged card was shaking under her nose.

"For chrissakes, Lou, knock it off. A *greener* like
her, what does she know?" The fat man was smiling,
reached out to touch her shoulder, and she withdrew.

"Okay, okay. Little lady in the nice pretty clothes,

get this straight. Nothing against you. Nothing against your people. But you see, the meat I sell means I can't sell milk, cheese, sour cream—nothing like that. Now you go across the street to the German. That nice German fella will sell you a ton of cheesecake.''

"That *chazer*," said the fat man.

Dimple ran from the store, eyes closed, hands covering her mouth and nostrils.

On the stroll home with Meena she thought of Lake Market, where twenty hawkers would be grabbing at her for any small change she had. They'd do anything to please her, cut a tangerine in half if she had only ten *paise*. What was wrong with her money? In Calcutta she'd buy from Muslims, Biharis, Christians, Nepalis. She was used to many races; she'd never been a communalist. And so long as she had money to spend no one would ask her what community she belonged to. She was caught in the crossfire of an American communalism she couldn't understand. She felt she'd come very close to getting killed on her third morning in America.

The next evening they went to a party in Manhattan near Columbia University. Archana was carried in her summer pajamas, since baby sitters were expensive and not to be trusted.

"A Punjabi fellow," said Jyoti in the car, "but you'll like him. I bought the sofa from his cousin."

"We socialize quite a bit," Meena said to Dimple. "There are lots of Indians here. Too many, in fact."

"I hope the Mullicks will be there tonight. You'll like them. He started out working for the city, then he started his own consulting firm. *Mint*ing money. And Ina is very smart and very pretty."

"She wears pants and mascara. You know the type," said Meena.

The party at Vinod Khanna's was big and noisy. The Mullicks were not there. The men smelled of after-shave lotion. The women wore a lot of gold with their expensive silk saris. Dimple was glad she'd worn the best she had. They spoke English with each other, but now and then exploded into excited Bengali or Hindi, and laughed very loudly.

"How long have you been here?" Vinod Khanna asked Dimple. He'd come over as a student, done a business degree at N.Y.U., then opened an import-export business. He had a handsome baby face, flabby muscles, flashy clothes. Jyoti had said that Vinod was doing very well, with three boutiques in the Village and a trading company. When, in answer to his question, Dimple said, "Three or four days," he said he'd thought she looked fresh and un-Americanized. "After you get settled and if you're looking for a job, give me a ring. We can always use salesgirls." Amit was at her side in a flash, his light wool Bargat Ali suit looking drab and wrinkled next to all the double-knits. "One breadwinner in the family is quite enough," said Amit, looking to Dimple for agreement. When she smiled, he added, "Besides, Dimple can't add two and two. She would ruin your business in a fortnight."

"Still—" said Vinod Khanna, "many Indian wives find it relaxing to work. Now come meet my roommate, Kiran Mehra. He was in Calcutta for three years." But just as they started following him across the room, Vinod Khanna caught the eye of a tall young woman tightly wrapped in magenta silk. He left Dimple and Amit and dashed to her side. Amit went to the kitchen to get more ice. Meena Sen materialized at Dimple's elbow and whispered that the girl in magenta was Miss

Chakravorty, a physics student at Columbia who lived at the international center. "She goes out with any and everyone, even Africans!"

Dimple tried to smile brightly and look happy. She found an armchair in one corner and spoke only when people came up to her and addressed her so directly that she couldn't pretend they were talking to others behind her. "When did you arrive?" or "Have you been in New York long?" or worse still, "What does your husband do?" But when she said, "Two days; I've been here two days," they stopped listening to her, as if her opinions didn't matter. One woman she met, a Mrs. Bhattacharya from New Jersey, had been in the States for sixteen years and two months. She wore a green and white checkered sari, like a tablecloth.

Dimple worked her nervous fingers on the pretty paper napkin she had been given with her Coca-Cola on the rocks, and before she knew it the napkin was in tiny shreds. All around her people looked happy.

"They are so dirty," Mrs. Sen was saying to Mrs. Bhattacharya. "They bathe only once a week. Rest of the week they just take two-minute showers and use a lot of perfume. I don't want Archana to learn bad ways."

"What I can't stand," said Mrs. Bhattacharya, "is washing clothes in the bathroom sink. Have you seen that? They brush their teeth and spit in that bowl, and then they wash their clothes in the same bowl. I find it quite unforgivable." Though she spoke in Bengali, Dimple noticed, Mrs. Bhattacharya's rhythm was all wrong. Dimple crunched a piece of ice between her teeth and said very quietly to the other women, "But we're terribly dirty too. I mean people . . ." She hesitated to say anything gross, then remembered a faded

signboard by the Dhakuria Lakes—COMMITTING NUI-
SANCE IS STRICKLY PROHIBITED—and completed her
sentence rather breathlessly. "I mean we don't think
anything of committing nuisance in public. Even well-
dressed people commit nuisance on the streets." But
she knew they had stopped listening; among themselves, India could do no wrong.

She heard Vinod Khanna say at her elbow, "I don't
think I got around to introducing Kiran. Come this instant." The roommate was squatting on the rug near
Miss Chakravorty's pillows—for a crazy moment she
wondered if he was going to commit nuisance—his shirt
now open down to the middle of his chest revealing too
much curly black hair and the top of a blue undershirt.
A *blue* undershirt! She had not seen anything so sophisticated before coming to New York. "Lovely place,
Calcutta," he said absent-mindedly. "A little hard to
get around in, but swinging, real swinging." Then
Kiran Mehra, his long hair curling over the edge of his
floral collar and his tummy unnaturally flat inside the
gay checkered pants, inched closer to Miss Chakravorty.

"You're a meany, yes you are, a real meany monster," Miss Chakravorty giggled to a man standing over
her. "I said a very *wet* martini. Do you want to get me
in trouble?"

"What is there to worry, Miss Chakravorty? I'll see
you home." The man was mustached and middle-aged
with wispy sideburns just beginning to gray. His mustache curled down toward his chin, making his mouth
seem small and insincere. He wore a pink shirt and an
ascot, but there were rings of dark pink moisture under
his arms. He pressed the martini closer to her; she
speared the olive, ate it, dull green against her dazzling
teeth, then tucked the toothpick behind the man's half-

hidden ear. Kiran Mehra, still watching intently, made his way to the kitchen.

"I have to be back by twelve-thirty, Mr. Desai," the girl in magenta said. "That's far too early for *you*!" She sipped from the glass and let the tip of her little pink tongue slither impudently over her high-gloss lips. That small gesture reminded Dimple of Hindi film actresses, but the setting was not lavish enough for a Bombay extravaganza. She realized suddenly that she had expected apartments in America to resemble the sets in a Raj Kapoor movie: living rooms in which the guests could break into song and dance, winding carpeted staircases, sunken swimming pools, billiard tables, roulette wheels, baby grand pianos, bars and velvet curtains. This apartment was barely the size of the Basus' on Dr. Sarat Banerjee Road.

"Let's eat," Vinod Khanna shouted from the kitchen. "The food'll get cold."

The dining area was set apart from the living room by a bookcase. The floor there was not carpeted and bore signs of curry spillage. The oval dining table was covered by an Indian hand-loomed bedspread. Stacks of china and plastic plates were on one side; also glasses, paper napkins and four sets of knives, forks, spoons. Kiran Mehra was still bringing out the food from the narrow galley of a kitchen. It reminded Dimple of a jumbo jet's galley, with its warming oven set high in the wall. A plate of mutton *biriyani* rice was already on the table. It was garnished with crisply fried onion rings and little brown things that Mrs. Sen explained were sautéed mushrooms. On his next trip, Kiran Mehra wore a bright yellow apron that reached to his knees, and balanced a huge casserole dish of mutton *do-piaza* in one hand and a platter of reddish chicken parts in the other. Just like a stewardess, Dim-

ple thought. The legend on his apron said A KISS IS MY
REWARD.

"Come *on*, everybody," Vinod Khanna was still
shouting, though only Miss Chakravorty and two Punjabi attendants were left on the cushions near the stereo.
"The food's getting cold."

"Chicken *tandoori*!" cried Mrs. Bhattacharya. "You
people from the North really know how to cook!" A
chorus of praise for Punjabi cooking, Punjabi prosper-
ity, Punjabi self-reliance, followed from the various
Bengalis present.

"Well, it's broiled," Kiran conceded. "I can't make
tandoori without the right oven, but we try our best,
we make do . . ." He looked very happy, and thrust
two chicken legs and half a breast on Mrs. Bhattacharya's plate.

"We make do . . ." was like a refrain, Dimple
thought, as she sat on a ladderback chair by the kitchen
wall and picked her way through the rice and spicy
mutton.

"Those who want to be big *sahebs* can use knives
and forks," Vinod was shouting. "The rest of us will
use our fingers and eat Indian style."

"I see only legs and breasts," whispered Dimple to
Jyoti Sen, when he came by to fill the ladies' Coke
glasses. "What happened to the rest of the chicken?
Did they throw it out?"

He laughed so hard at her question that his eyes almost disappeared in little rolls of fat. Dimple cursed
herself for asking, even for noticing. He explained,
though she no longer cared, that chicken parts came in
clean little plastic packages and that one didn't have to
buy any parts that one didn't want.

"Miss Chakravorty," called Kiran Mehra, "you can't
let me down. You must assess my culinary effort."

"I really can't," said the girl in magenta. "I'm dieting. Do you know I've put on five kilos in all the wrong places since my last vacation back home? But I'm sure it's all terribly good." She crinkled up her nose and looked adorable.

Mrs. Bhattacharya, who was standing in front of Dimple and slurping up rice by the fingerful, muttered something about stupid modern girls who diet until they look skinny and haggard. "The food is so good, so *unadulterated* here, and these girls don't want to eat! I find it quite unforgivable." Another Bengali woman in pearl and gold drop-earrings remarked that she could make better chicken curry here because the quality of chicken was so much better than back home. "Our chickens are so scrawny," she said. "If the farmer can't eat himself, how can he feed his chickens, I ask you?" Her earrings shook with passion.

"You're exaggerating, Mrs. Chakladar," admonished an older man in a dark business suit. "You have not been here as long as Mrs. Bhattacharya and myself, but let us assure you that though our chickens may be smaller and thinner they taste far, far better." Everyone agreed with him, and Mrs. Chakladar chewed a drumstick in apologetic gloom. Mrs. Sen added that, talking of taste, didn't they all find the unhomogenized milk back home tastier, somehow. In the kitchen, Kiran and another young man were making coffee and discussing the humanizing qualities of songs and lyrics by S. D. Burman. "He's so sincere," Kiran said with feeling. "Burman-*saab* makes me want to cry. I can listen to him for hours." Dimple learned, to her dismay, that Hindi films were sometimes shown in high-school auditoriums in Queens by the Indo-American Society, on Saturday nights or Sunday mornings. Bengali films were intellectual and played for the college students; Satyajit

Ray might be fun back home, said Meena Sen, but here his films were too sad. The subtitles made them foreign, and the Americans laughed at all the wrong places.

At a quarter to midnight, Kiran played the soundtrack of *Anuraag*. "Such sincerity, such feeling," everyone said. They sat around on the floor, the men with coffee cups in front of them. Among the women only the girl in magenta took coffee, and she took it black. At a quarter to one, she sang two songs from *Anuraag* herself, then waited modestly for the compliments. Most of the men said she should be in the movies; the women said she sang quite sweetly. "Oh, my God," the girl squealed, looking at her watch, "I should have been back twenty minutes ago. They'll throw me out! I won't have a place to sleep tonight!" The hairy and ascoted Mr. Desai jumped to his feet and gave her his arm with self-conscious gallantry.

"Ushakantbhai, it'll be terribly out of your way," said Mrs. Bhattacharya severely. "Mr. Bhattacharya and I will drop her." But Ushakant Desai had already collected Miss Chakravorty's fake fur coat from the bedroom and was propelling her to the front door.

"Next Saturday at my place," he said from the doorway. "I'll call you later in the week. See you. *Namaste*." Before the front door shut behind him, Dimple saw a barefoot blond girl from the apartment across the hall, smiling mysteriously, walk out with a cat on a red leash.

"Such a warm night and that girl is wearing a fur coat," Mrs. Bhattacharya exploded.

On the drive back to Queens, Jyoti said wasn't it wonderful that Indians abroad were so outgoing and open-minded. They didn't give a damn about communalism and petty feelings. They personally counted a number of Punjabis and Gujaratis and some South Indians among their friends. Jyoti told Dimple not to restrict herself to Bengalis, or else she'd miss a lot of the experience of being abroad. ''I mean I can honestly say that I'm as close to Vinod and Kiran as I am to any boys in Calcutta. And at work there's even a Pak boy in the office. No trouble whatsoever. Here we are all the same people, isn't that so?''

''The Mullicks should have been there,'' said Meena. ''They've never missed a party at Vinod's. I'd better give them a call tomorrow and see what's wrong.'' Archana woke up very suddenly and Meena tried to rock her back to sleep.

''Bijoy Mullick will be a useful contact for you, Amit. He might give you a job lead and things. He used to work for the city till he got smart. But Ina Mullick might give Dimple some bad ideas.''

Dimple did not want to think about job leads yet. ''What do you mean 'bad ideas'? I'm almost twenty-one, aren't I?''

''I don't even want to say,'' Jyoti replied. ''Bijoy is my friend, and Ina isn't really bad. But I will tell you this—she chain-smokes.''

''She's more American than the Americans,'' said Meena, while changing a diaper in the front seat.

''I blame Bijoy, personally,'' said Jyoti. ''When a woman starts going wrong, it's usually because her husband didn't look after her enough. He started that business and got too busy; then she had all that money.''

''I hear she wants to stay,'' said Meena. ''She was always wanting to go back to Calcutta when we knew them in Queens. Then they moved to Manhattan and now she says she's happy here.''

''She started going to school at nights,'' said Jyoti.

''She met bad types,'' said Meena.

"You mean you can go to college at night?" asked Dimple.

"If you want to get mugged on the subway," said Jyoti.

"I blame Bijoy," said Meena.

"Jyoti's right," said Amit. "With so many Indians around and a television and a child, a woman shouldn't have any time to get crazy ideas." He looked to Dimple for confirmation; she realized the conversation had been going in a four-cornered game and it was her turn.

"You're so lucky that Archana can sleep through parties like that," said Dimple. She didn't want to think of the Mullicks and the terrifying Ina. The last few days had been so pleasant; she had felt so much more alert than she had in the flat on Dr. Sarat Banerjee Road. She had been so certain that Amit's intelligence and integrity would be magically rewarded by first-rate jobs that she did not want to have to visualize the actual process of circling ads, ironing shirts, putting on a tie and jacket, and interviewing bosses. Tonight, she'd started to doubt again. Amit had not looked self-assured. Among the men, he'd looked frail. She'd seen other men avoid him.

"When I get a job," Amit said to Jyoti, "I'll throw the grandest party yet. With the first paycheck. I mean it, old boy."

"Remember, that's a promise," Jyoti laughed. "You have three and a half witnesses."

The man on TV was called Captain Kangaroo, and he was very fat. But light on his feet. Dimple thought it was safe to assume most fat men were light on their feet. She told Archana that, but Archana did not want to watch Captain Kangaroo walk lightly on his feet. She

spread wet sheets of paper on the floor and fingerpainted.

"I can't stand to watch her fingerpaint," Meena said
in English. "It's so messy. But here they say it's good
for children. It makes them less inhibited." She vacu-
umed and dusted around Dimple and Archana.

"I never fingerpainted as a child, did you?"

"Of course not," said Dimple.

When she had finished cleaning, Meena set up an
ironing board in front of the TV. She had a pretty aqua
and white, Teflon-coated iron. Dimple decided she
would buy a pretty iron like that when she had her own
place, except that she was not sure the Teflon coating
was a good idea. It could get scratched, and in India
she probably could not get it recoated.

"Please let me help," Dimple pleaded.

"Oh, no, there's nothing to it."

She ironed three shirts, two pillowcases and one cotton sari. The sari was hard to manage. Halfway she
gave up and rested on the sofa beside Dimple. "If it
wasn't for backaches, I'd love being pregnant."

Dimple tried not to look at the huge stomach. Meena
put her feet up on the coffee table and gave Dimple
household hints: wash saris in the bathtub, throw them
in the dryer, fold them in half and use spray starch.
"But if the washing machine is in the basement of the
building, let Amit do the laundry."

Dimple laughed at the suggestion. "I'm sure he
wouldn't do the laundry! He hasn't washed a hanky in
his life. I wouldn't let him."

"You want to get mugged? Women in *this* building—
not me, touch wood—have been mugged in the basement. If you want to get killed and worse things, then
go do the laundry yourself. Don't listen to me. I tell
you these people are *goondas*."

"But why would anyone want to mug *me*?"

"It's all the rare beef they eat. It makes them crazy."

At ten to one, Amit came in carrying a newspaper under his arm and four cheese Danishes. He pushed the plastic flowers to one side and put the greasy bag of Danishes on top of the bookcase. "Aren't you going to ask me where I went?" he asked Dimple.

"Where did you go?"

"It's no good if I have to tell you to ask me."

Meena Sen quickly went into the kitchen, taking the little girl with her, and banged pans around to provide the Basus some privacy.

"No one appreciates me," Amit said.

"But I didn't want to ask you in case you didn't want to be asked."

"I hope you like chicken gumbo soup," Meena shouted from the kitchen.

"But you should have known that I'd want you to ask me where I'd been."

On TV, which no one had remembered to turn off, a man in a striped jacket was giving away a refrigerator-freezer, a washer-dryer and a skiing trip to the Andes.

A viewer sent in a question: what is the best exercise in the world? Dimple heard the pretty hostess say tentatively: yoga or swimming. Then the guest doctor broke in and said: no, lady, sex is what you mean. Well-executed, it employs more muscles than the butterfly stroke. Dimple could have watched television all day. Another viewer sent in a household hint: bake bananas in empty, cleaned-out TV-dinner trays, then freeze and reheat them as necessary.

Meena Sen spent most of the day in bed because of her backache. She did not want the TV to be rolled into the bedroom. Archana liked to sit on the floor of the bedroom near her mother and tear old newspapers. "We call her our shredding machine," Meena said with a laugh, but Dimple could tell she was suffering.

Dimple liked having the living room to herself. She kept the TV on all day and did odd jobs like cleaning windows and vacuuming. Cleaning windows was easy with the spray cans of foaming ammonia: the grime that rubbed off on the paper towel made her feel good. In Calcutta, though the servant swept and wet-ragged the floor twice a day, he never worked above ankle level. The tops of the fan blades would hold an oily accumulation half an inch thick. The tops of the wardrobes had never been dusted. She'd never seen a vacuum cleaner before coming over; the noise, the little light that wormed its way under the sofa, the sharp little cough as it swallowed lint, cookie crumbs and paper shreds all made her feel more powerful than she had ever felt. She stared at the clean, wide sidewalks, the roads stretching in every direction, children on bicycles, old people shuffling, the occasional delivery man, and wondered what Amit was doing in the city. He was angry all the time. She was glad he was out so much; it was easier to think of him, even get sentimental over him, when he was not in the room. He had never voted. He was ticklish just above the knees. He liked trams but did not like buses. Onions made him belch. At age sixteen he had written five poems. Those details had not seemed important before, but now she felt it helped explain the man who strode out of the building every morning at nine-thirty and wouldn't be back until six-fifteen.

At lunch time, now that Meena could not get out of bed too easily, she made sandwiches for all three and brought them into the bedroom. Archana would not sit beside her on the floor; she dropped her crumbs on the bedspread and held her mother's hand whenever Dimple smiled and tried to say something funny. Dimple wished she could be out in the living room watching daytime shows with inspiring names like "The Guiding Light" and "Love of Life." The women on television led complicated lives, became pregnant frequently and under suspicious circumstances (but were never huge or tired like Meena Sen), murdered or were murdered, were brought to trial and released; they suffered through the Ping-Pong volley of their fates with courage. But they hardly ever talked to children. She could not learn from them how to make friends with Archana though she learned the details of American home life. For instance, everything she saw on TV was about love; even murder and death were love gone awry. But all she read in the newspapers was about death, the scary, ugly kind of death, random and poorly timed. Dimple much preferred to watch TV than read. And she gave up trying to make friends with children.

Amit came back in twenty minutes carrying six cheese Danishes. "I didn't expect you back so early," Dimple said. "Shall I make you a sandwich?"

"You don't sound happy to see me back," Amit said and bit moodily into a Danish.

"All I meant was should I make lunch for you?"

"What kind of a question is that?"

"I meant are you staying or going out again?" She took the bread knife out of the drawer. "Let me fix something while you decide."

"No, forget it," Amit said. "I wouldn't eat it even if you made it." He flipped channels on TV until he found an old Western movie, then sat on the floor with the bag of cheese Danishes.

* * *

Jyoti got Ina Mullick on the fifth try and Ina said why didn't they come over for dinner that evening since they were having a few people over anyway. Dimple asked Meena if she should wear a silk sari or would a cotton do, and Meena said she herself was going to wear cotton because the Mullicks were informal.

"Ina Mullick will probably wear pants," Jyoti laughed. Then added in a loud whisper to Amit, "She's a red hot number," which the women were supposed to hear but ignore.

"Don't pay any attention to him," Meena said to Dimple. "He's always saying nasty things about her."

The Mullicks lived in an apartment complex on the corner of 100th Street and Central Park West. Negro policemen with dogs walked around the building and playground. Dimple said she was scared of the policemen; they just did not look inoffensive, like the ones back home.

They could hear a party in progress even when they were in the elevator. In the hall, the music kept getting louder. All Western music, raucous singing. Dimple was already sorry she'd come. Her English had grown less confident since she'd arrived in America.

Ina Mullick opened the front door after two rings. She squinted a split second—Dimple could read disappointment in those large eyes behind the smoke-colored glasses. Then she smiled. "Hello, Meena, Jyoti. My God, promise not to have the baby *here*, okay?" Jyoti introduced the Basus.

Dimple could not take her eyes off Ina Mullick. She was wearing white pants and a printed shirt that ended in a large knot. There was an isosceles triangle of hard flesh between the shirt and waistband of her pants, with a dimpled navel in the center. Dimple had no idea that skinniness could look so chillingly sexy on some people. "It's very kind of you to invite us," Dimple said in Bengali.

"Not at all," Ina laughed. "We love to show off." She blew cigarette smoke through her nostrils and led them into the living room. Her lipstick was the brightest red Dimple had ever seen. Amit seemed uncomfortable; he walked around the room staring at the Kangra prints and mildewed wooden goddesses mounted on silk and dramatically lighted. There was a deep, long aquarium on top of a low bookcase; Dimple tapped the glass in front of a tiny, shark-shaped fish that was staring at her, but Ina said, "It's a one-way glass, the lucky devils." Ina took her hand. "Come along and meet the others," she said brightly. Dimple would have preferred to watch the fish.

There were already a dozen people in the apartment—it was the largest she'd yet seen in New York—and not all the guests were Indian. There was a blond woman in clothes that rivaled Ina's (but not with the same effect) who seemed to be married to a short, wide-shouldered Indian. But there were also two unattached *sahebs*, unless two of the docile, seated Indian women could have been their wives (a possibility Dimple immediately dismissed). One, bearded and graying, was talking about Kangra art with Amit, who admitted he knew nothing about it. Amit was running his finger around the rim of his collar.

Bijoy Mullick did not seem to go with Ina. A bald, spidery man, he looked like a postal clerk, the holder of a very low desk job in some enormous Calcutta office. Dimple could imagine him in a *dhoti* stepping with sockless shoes around monsoon puddles, but she could not imagine him as an engineer, a rich America-settled businessman who probably bossed *saheb* engineers around and had a wife who dressed like a cabaret dancer. She could not imagine treating him as a man who could help her husband find a job.

"Please, please, sit here," he said to Dimple, giving up his chair near the color TV. "It is only a silly game; I will turn off the sound." Dimple sat and watched men in white uniforms dancing over the greenest possible grass. It was like watching the fish in the aquarium. She wished Amit could get away from the *saheb* with a beard and sit in the armchair and discuss job leads with Bijoy Mullick, but she was too shy to move. Ina brought her a Seven-Up in a blue glass with ice cubes and a twist of lemon. Jyoti and Amit, each with Scotch and soda, hovered closer to the chair. Bijoy took the hassock and sat absorbed in his game.

"Well, Dimple," said Ina, as she sat on the edge of the coffee table nearly at Dimple's elbow, "what do you do all day? You must be bored out of your skull."

Dimple flushed with anger. I am *not* bored, she thought defiantly.

"Don't teach her all your Women's Lib stuff!" Jyoti laughed. "Amit, I warned you! Time to save your wife!"

"Oh, go to hell," Ina snapped, and the men stayed back, joking among themselves. "You've got to crack the whip, don't you think? Or do they have you branded?"

"You have a very lovely apartment, Mrs. Mullick. I've never seen statues mounted on walls before."

"What you see," said Ina Mullick almost sternly, "is a perfectly normal apartment that I'm frankly getting a little tired of, in a part of Manhattan that is neither safe nor convenient. We are trying to live like anyone else with minimum good taste and a comfortable income. I could leave it tomorrow."

Bijoy turned and said, "Ina has this theory about

Indian immigrants. It takes them a year to get India out of their system. In the second year they've bought all the things they've hungered for. So then they go back, or they stay here and vegetate or else they've got to live here like anyone else.'' Dimple found she could not really listen to such a strange-looking man with such a high-pitched voice.

''My big crisis came at the end of two months, Biju,'' Ina said. Then she laughed a tinkly little laugh and Bijoy lit her new cigareete. Dimple was amazed that the triangle of flesh didn't crease as she sat; her thighs didn't flare where they folded over the table edge. ''Actually, I looked a lot like you. I married Biju from a doctored picture and didn't really get a good look at him until I was on a plane for New York.''

''By then it was too late,'' Bijoy giggled.

''Who are the other people?'' Dimple asked.

''The *sahebs*, you mean,'' said Ina with a snicker. ''Old friends, some associates of Biju's . . . a couple of tennis-playing friends of mine. Have you met Prodosh and Marsha Mookerji, by the way?''

''No,'' said Dimple.

''What does he do?'' asked Jyoti.

''He teaches at N.Y.U. A very, very brilliant boy. Studied at Yale and married a teacher.''

''A *memsaheb*?'' asked Dimple.

''Which Mookerji family is this?'' asked Amit.

''Good God!'' cried Ina Mullick.

''Very sorry, very sorry. I didn't mean . . .''

''She *is a memsaheb*, Dimple, but it's time to start thinking of them as Americans. Marsha and Prodosh are my two favorite people in New York. *Now*—would you like another Seven-Up, or could I tempt you to have a gin and lime?''

"She doesn't like alcoholic beverages," Amit said. "She doesn't even like Coke."

"*I* didn't like gin until I tried it, if you can believe that," Ina Mullick answered. Amit retired a few steps to joke with Meena and Jyoti. "Then I knew why the men at these parties were always a damn sight happier than their goody-goody wives. Jyoti—" she called, "how would you feel after four Seven-Ups? Pissed, right? How about it, Dimple? A weak gin?"

She felt that Amit was waiting for just the right answer, that it was up to her to uphold Bengali womanhood, marriage and male pride. The right answer, *I do not need stimulants to feel happy in my husband's presence . . . my obligation is to my husband,* seemed to dance before her eyes as though it were printed on a card. All she had to do was read it, but she feared Ina's laughter, or anger, more than anything in the world. If she took a drink she knew Amit would write it to his mother and his mother would call the Dasguptas and accuse them of raising an immoral, drunken daughter. The Calcutta rumor mill operated as effectively from New York as it did from Park Street.

"Maybe a very weak one, next time," she said.

A few minutes later Dimple was startled by two loud kicks at the door. She thought it had to be the police; she'd seen *The French Connection* in Calcutta as part of her preparation for New York, and kicking in the door seemed to be the way police entered apartments in New York. She clutched the arm of the chair. She did not want to be deported. The music seemed suddenly louder as everyone stopped talking. Ina opened the door as far as the chain allowed, then closed it, dropped the chain and opened it wide.

Three people entered: a tall young Bengali in aviator glasses, navy blue turtleneck sweater and white pants;

a slightly taller *memsaheb*, dark-haired with dark-framed glasses in a gray pantsuit and a white turtleneck sweater. But Dimple couldn't take her eyes off the enormous young *saheb* who'd entered with them: as tall as the door frame, in blue jeans and a white shirt, with an unbuttoned, unmatching vest from a pinstriped three-piece suit. His hair was a mass of tight black curls, tumbling over his ears, neck and forehead. When he saw Ina he almost growled, "Ina Mullick, you super-fine Bengali *piece*!" He clamped two enormous paws on her white-trousered bottom and lifted her to his level. "Where's that bald-headed freak of a husband of yours?" Ina Mullick looked no larger than a child in his arms. Dimple's fingers were digging into the chair; she was afraid there would be shooting. Bijoy Mullick rose slowly from the hassock in front of the television and made his way to the kitchen. "There he is! Bijoy, come out and fight like a man! No hiding behind the pots and pans."

"He's gone to get you a beer," said Ina Mullick. She planted a long, loud kiss on his cheek.

"Why didn't you say you were getting a beer? Hey, Bijoy, never mind." He lifted Ina even higher, like a young fathering admiring his baby, then lowered her slowly and let her drop the last foot and a half.

Bijoy emerged with two beers, one can extended, one already poured into a glass. "I thought you'd done me a favor," he said. He came up to the young man's armpits. "Here's courage," he said.

Ina strolled with the tall young woman and the two young men over to Dimple's corner. She found herself retreating in the chair.

"*These* are the Mookerjis," she said. "Prodosh and Marsha. The young gorilla is Milt Glasser, who probably shocked half the ladies here out of their petticoats with that performance.'' But before the young American could be properly introduced, he spotted the television and squatted on the floor in front of it. The boy's hair and head covered nearly all of the screen. Bijoy sat on the hassock; they exchanged some baseball information and then were quiet. Surprisingly, Milt Glasser had a soft, gentle voice.

Marsha Mookerji sat on the arm of Dimple's chair and pointed to the young man with the toe of her shoe. ''If this is the first time you've seen Milt and Ina, you're probably wondering what that was all about.''

''Your vodka collins, Marsha,'' said Prodosh, handing her a tall, tinkling drink. He was carrying a beer for himself. Dimple had never heard of a host not making the drinks. She thought it quite unforgivable, especially from people who thought they were so sophisticated.

''Another Scotch?'' Prodosh took Amit's glass and went back to the kitchen; Amit followed.

''He's my baby brother,'' said Marsha Mookerji. ''Twenty-three years old and still growing.'' Dimple had trouble spotting a likeness. Marsha, though she was taller than Amit and maybe as tall as Jyoti, was delicately built, with a face that Dimple thought of as intelligent before she could assess its beauty. Even this was troubling. Dimple had been brought up to think of women only as beautiful, pretty, or good mothers. Marsha was fair, tall and slim—the prerequisites for Indian beauty—but excessively so. Intelligent, then friendly. About prettiness, she couldn't decide.

''Mr. Mullick tells me you are a schoolteacher,'' said Amit as he came back to the room, sipping his new drink. Prodosh stood beside him.

''Bijoy, you mean? Yes, I teach.''

"That's good," said Amit. "It gives you something to do."

"Do you have things to do, Mrs. Basu?" Marsha asked.

"I've only been here a week." She thought for a moment of the job she'd been offered by Vinod Khanna. How nice it would be to say, "Of course it's only a small thing and it doesn't interfere with my *real* job, but I have a small job in the Village (wherever and whatever a 'village' meant in this country), showing off our Indian crafts . . ." And Amit could say, "It's good for a woman to get out of the apartment for a few hours a week." She pictured herself in a bright sari showing Indian brass to friendly people like Marsha Mookerji.

"Have you been to Calcutta?" asked Amit.

"If Prodosh ever goes back, I'll go along."

"He doesn't go?"

"He hasn't been in six years. He's afraid he couldn't adjust now, so we bring his parents over every summer. He's the only son, so it works out."

Dimple wanted to ask if his parents had objected. She could imagine the bitterness of Prodosh Mookerji's parents: a brilliant and handsome only son, foreign-trained and foreign-employed. He could have brought a fortune into the family. What a selfish thing to do, make a love-match with this enormous, friendly, American schoolteacher. If she, Dimple Dasgupta, had not been good enough for Amit Basu of Dr. Sarat Banerjee Road, what kind of woman would have done for Prodosh Mookerji? She could imagine the suicide threats of the mother, disinheritance by the father, the kind of perpetual gloom that an ungrateful Bengali son can cast on the last years of his parents' life. She hated Prodosh Mookerji with a rage that made her shake. But how could she ask this smiling *memsaheb* in the dark glasses:

Excuse me, Mrs. Mookerji. Were your parents-in-law deeply disappointed when they saw you?

"Do you teach in the neighborhood?" she asked.

"I teach at Barnard," she said.

"But that's a college," said Amit.

"We're exceptionally lucky that we both have university jobs in Manhattan," she explained. "We met in graduate school and got our Ph.D.s together."

"You mean you're a lady professor?" asked Amit.

"Just a professor," she said.

Suddenly Milt punched off the TV and announced to no one in particular, "That's it everyone. Mets Win. Seaver Whitewashes Hapless Padres. Fans Fourteen. Claims Twelfth Victory. Bijoy, want a beer?" He crushed his empty beer can in his hand. "I prefer ice hockey," said Bijoy. Milt took Bijoy's empty glass with him. On his way to the kitchen he looked down at his sister and Dimple, smiled, then stomped off. Dimple had never seen such large boots.

Amit went to the kitchen. Dimple had finished her Seven-Up. She asked Marsha Mookerji—Doctor Marsha Glasser Mookerji, Associate Professor of Semitic Studies, who'd just done a series of television broadcasts on Channel Thirteen on the Arab-Israeli War, the oil embargo, on the personalities of Arab and Israeli leaders—if her college took evening students who were trying to complete their B.A.s. She asked her about the safety of the subways. She admitted she'd never understood politics, but that India was on the Arabs' side and America was on Israel's side; which side was right? Dimple said she wished that India would do something that would make the world respect it again.

Ina Mullick brought Bijoy his glass of beer, but held it away from him as he reached. "Time to light the hibachi, darling." She was wearing an apron over her white pants and shirt. The apron said LOVE ME LOVE MY COOKING.

In a corner between the dining table and the stereo, Milt Glasser was talking to Amit and the wide-shouldered Indian about Alice Cooper and Deca-Rock. Ina Mullick carried platters full of chicken parts marinating in yoghurt. "I think your husband is going to get sick," she giggled on her way past Dimple. Dimple walked over to Amit and heard Milt describe some show in which the performer chopped heads off dolls on stage. She watched the fish, furious at their ignorance of being watched. When she looked up again, Milt was carrying a thick platter of red, bloody beef out to the porch. "All you beaf-eating Hindus that want steak, come and cook it yourself!" he called. She watched in horror as Bijoy used the same long-handled fork for both the beef and the chicken. She went to the kitchen for another Seven-Up. Milt was back, talking to the bearded *saheb* and Prodosh Mookerji. "I was just a kid when the first Kennedy got it," he was saying. "And when King and Bobby got killed I was a senior in high school. But when Roberto Clemente died in that crash I was a senior at Columbia and I couldn't eat for three days. There I was on New Year's Day in my room, *crying*. Christ!" Dimple couldn't follow the way he talked, the things he talked about and the amazing leaps between his conversations. When he spotted her just outside the kitchen with a tall empty glass in her hand, he took one giant step toward her, clamped his hands on her bare midriff and lifted her onto the plastic counter. "*Now*, Mrs. Dimple Basu," he said, "I am going to fix you my sister's favorite drink. The nice thing about vodka is that your husband will never know."

* * *

On the drive home, Amit said, "It must all be black money. How else can you have things like that?"

"You're thinking like an Indian, Amit," said Jyoti. They had left early, since they were using another lady in the apartment building, a Gujarati whose husband was away on business, as a baby sitter.

Late that night when they were in the Sens' pull-out bed in Queens, Amit said to Dimple, "I screwed things up. You saw that for yourself. I couldn't even tell a joke."

Dimple said, "You don't need Bijoy Mullick and his connections. You'll get a job on your own."

Long after he'd fallen asleep, she could taste the beef blood in her mouth. The drink had been nice, but she'd fought back sickness when she saw the fork holes in the chicken.

Dimple was reading a letter from Pintu that said that Mrs. Basu had fallen in the bathroom and had fractured her ankle and the servant had gone home to the village for a month, but Dimple was thinking how nice it would be to have her own apartment when Amit found a job.

She played a game: she took two pieces of paper and wrote MANHATTAN on one and QUEENS on the other, folded both, then picked up one of them with her eyes shut. She usually picked MANHATTAN.

Jyoti said, "The problem isn't that A killed B while waiting to fill up his gas tank, but that A had a gun to kill with."

Dimple liked to hear the men talk while she helped Meena do the dishes. They had finished a late dinner of chicken curry and fried rice and the men had argued all through dinner about guns and licenses. Amit said,

"The question is, did B provoke A knowing that A had a gun in the glove compartment."

Dimple felt better than she had since coming to the States. She thought she had never really been friends with anyone before this, never stayed with someone for weeks and discussed important things like love and death. That's what America meant to her.

She heard Jyoti say, "That's not fair, Amit. You can't *speculate* on A's and B's motives; you've got to stick to facts."

And Amit said, "Okay, Jyoti old boy, let's zero in on the gun. Let's confine ourselves for the moment to the instrument."

Dimple tried to find a dry spot in her dishcloth and wondered why all Jyoti's conversations led back to violence. Muggings, rape, murder: they were remote and exotic, even a little exciting on TV, but when Jyoti described them they became ugly and accessible. As if he did not know that the battered-handsome detective-hero would make an exciting, timely appearance. Jyoti always looked so earnest and vulnerable when he talked of muggings that she wanted to comfort him, to tell him that victims always escaped with nothing worse than bruises.

Jyoti said in a querulous voice, "The gun is the *whole* problem. There's no need to go any further. It's only the gun we have to eliminate."

So, Dimple thought, he was in favor of gun-licensing. She liked to squirrel away information about Jyoti Sen. He was against mercy-killing. He liked to sleep till one o'clock in the afternoon on Sundays, then watch a game on television while reading the incredibly thick Sunday paper, then nap till dinner time. Sunday nights were the time for long conversations. Amit would drop off at midnight, but they couldn't open up the sofa until Jyoti was ready to turn in. She thought marriage was a chancy business; it could easily have been Jyoti instead of Amit that she had married since both were of the same caste and both were engineers.

With her back to the men, Dimple said, "If A killed B because he was angry, then that makes sense. But if B provoked A because he *wanted* to be killed, then that doesn't make any sense at all."

"You stay out of this," Amit laughed. "What do you know about frontier justice?"

Meena said, "The answer to all this is that people here are too impatient. Do you know I read in the papers that a woman divorced her husband because he snored?"

"You snore," Jyoti said.

At three A.M. Dimple said, "You snore too." She had to say it three times before Amit was awake enough to hear what she said.

"You woke me up to tell me that I snore?" Amit turned over on his stomach and bunched the pillow under his face.

"No, I woke you up to tell you I'd like a queen-size bed when we move out." She stroked his back so he would not fall asleep before she had finished. "I'd like a large queen-size bed."

"What do you mean *large* queen-size? Queen-size is queen-size."

"You are picking on me again," Dimple said. When he scratched her back so she would not cry too loudly and wake the Sens, she said, "Even your hands are rough. I can tell you hate me from the way you're scratching my back. You've always hated me! I know you wanted to marry someone fat and fair like Meena Sen!"

"For God's sake!" exploded Amit. "My hands are rough because I've been dishwashing for the last two nights. I can't sit around this apartment doing nothing, can I?"

"How can you do that to me?" Dimple cried. She was sitting up in bed with her face on her drawn-up knees and beating Amit's back with her fists. "If you're washing dishes what does that make me? I married an engineer, don't forget."

Amit slept on the floor that night. The next night Dimple slept on the floor and Amit slept on the sofa-bed.

"We never go to the movies," Dimple said to Amit as she was getting dressed. She pleated her red cotton sari very carefully, threw the loose end over her left shoulder and patted her hair in place. She wanted to look her very best for Ina Mullick. Jyoti and Meena had invited them for dinner. They had kept it small so that Bijoy and Amit could talk about jobs. "The point is, I haven't seen anything since *The French Connection* at the Minerva when I went with Pixie Ray."

Amit was busy changing the bed back into a sofa. In the beginning it had been Dimple's job, but she had given it up because she said sofas were for people who had to get up early, drink coffee in clean shirts and take a subway somewhere. She preferred to lie in the sofa-bed watching television and reading magazines with a lot of pictures. That morning she had read, under a picture of a patio with sand-blasted panels, geraniums hanging from hooks and thickly cushioned banquettes: Throw out the junk. Cut out. Pare down, slice away.

"Except for the cushions," said Mrs. J. Thomas, the bronzed middle-aged woman sitting on a banquette in the picture. "I absolutely adore cushions, they're so

romantic! When I'm lonely I sit for hours surrounded
by cushions. They are so much more comforting than
chihuahuas or African violets.'' And the magazine
added in italics: *Express yourself in your surroundings.
Discover your own grand passion and indulge it to ex-
cess. Then simplify the rest, throw out, be ruthless.
That's the secret to happiness.*

Dimple realized suddenly that she hated the Sens'
apartment, hated the sofa-bed, the wall-to-wall rug. It
was not a happy place like Mrs. J. Thomas's patio. It
did not express anyone's personality; it was merely convenient.

"If it were *my* dinner party," Dimple said when Amit
had finished with the sofa, "I'd serve the food in the
patio." She looked up at him archly as he stood beside
her, his left hand absently brushing the buttons of his
fly, making sure that everything was in order. She
wished he would not do that, expecially when she was
talking to him of glamorous parties on patios. In the
first weeks of marriage Dimple had been embarrassed
by the fly when she was laundering or ironing his pants.
In Calcutta she had trained herself not to see his hand
(always the left) as it stopped carefully at each button,
then slid up and down a few times before hanging limply
at his side. But in New York these little gestures had
begun to irritate her. She wondered if minor irritations
accumulated over decades could erupt into the kind of
violence she read about in the papers, and talked about
with Jyoti Sen. To distract herself, she said a little too
forcefully, "I would read up recipes and make water-
cress soup. I would do wonders with two carrots and a
chicken. You know what I mean? Something daring and
glamorous.''

It had been better, she decided, on Dr. Sarat Banerjee Road where Amit had been the boss. There she had

experienced him in terms of permissions and restraints.
Here in New York, Amit seemed to have collapsed inwardly, to have grown frail and shabby. That was the
problem: he was shabby compared to the nicely suited
Jyoti Sen or the men pushing toothpaste and deodorant
on television. She did not trust him anymore, did not
trust his high-pitched *yes* and *no* which had once
seemed oracular, did not trust his white cotton shirts
with erect collars. She wanted Amit to be infallible,
intractable, godlike, but with boyish charm; wanted him
to find a job so that after a decent number of years he
could take his savings and retire with her to a three-
story house in Ballygunje Park. It would not be too
hard, Dimple thought, to persuade him to settle in Ballygunje rather than in Kalyani. Her charms were still
untested.

"If it were *my* party, I'd serve drinks indoors and
food on the patio. Or should it be food indoors and
drinks on the patio?"

"What porch? What patio?" Amit asked and threw
his balled-up dirty shirt on her lap. "Clean this."

Ina and Bijoy Mullick came to the Sens' apartment
casually dressed. Ina's simple cotton sari, on her,
looked elegant; she had changed glasses. "Tomorrow
I'm going to enter a Gloria Steinem look-alike con-
test," she said, and lit a cigarette.

"That's the film star, isn't it?" Dimple asked, not
looking at Amit because she knew he liked her to keep
quiet and not make a fool of herself.

"You are probably thinking of Gloria Swanson," Bijoy said. "This one's far more dangerous." He was
taking his jacket off, loosening his tie and staring at
Dimple.

The women set out cheese and crackers on the coffee
table, then went off into the bedroom to see a new sari

that Mrs. Sen's mother had sent her through a recently arrived immigrant engineer.

Dimple sat on the bed with the new sari in front of her. It was green silk, still in its Indian Silk Museum box. She remembered that shop perfectly; that was where she'd bought her wedding sari. Archana toddled around the room kicking a small rubber ball. Ina Mullick leaned against the cold radiator and stared at Dimple. She could sense she was being stared at without looking up at Ina. When Meena left the room to boil water for rice, Ina said, "What do you do all day?" which made Dimple blush.

"Lots of things," Dimple said softly. "I read a lot."

"Don't you ever go out?"

"I don't have to."

Archana seemed to like Ina Mullick more than she'd ever liked Dimple. She played at Ina's feet. "Did you read about the doctor in St. Louis who dresses up like a magician?" Ina asked.

Dimple thought it was an irrelevant question or perhaps a trap to test her and was working on a witty comeback when Ina Mullick began a long story about the doctor. It seemed that he was both a doctor and a certified magician and pulled balls out of his little patients' ears. Then Ina Mullick lunged forward, pinned Archana's wriggling little body with one hand and pulled the small rubber ball out of the child's left ear. "I always wanted to be a magician," she laughed, and released Archana who wanted the trick to be done all over again.

Archana began to whine because Ina would not pull the ball out of her ear a second time, so Dimple took her into the kitchen. Ina followed them.

"I'm sorry," Ina laughed. "The trick doesn't always

work. If I try it a second time, the ear comes off in my hand instead of the ball."

Meena lifted her little girl and set her on the counter and gave her an Oreo cookie to suck on.

"You shouldn't do that," Dimple said. "I could easily have lifted Archana."

The little girl stopped crying and pried open the two halves of the cookie and licked the filling inside. Meena said, "Did you know that you can keep cucumber crisp for days if you put it in a bowl of water with a piece of coal? I read it somewhere."

Ina said, "Don't you ever get tired of household hints?"

"But I like crisp cucumber!" Meena protested. "Do you know anyone who prefers soggy cucumbers?"

At dinner they all sat on the floor and ate with their fingers. The men were still talking of load centers and substations and line outage and high voltage power transmissions systems. Though watching television was slowly improving Dimple's English, it still sounded like a foreign language to her. "I didn't think it would take so long," she said to Meena in the kitchen. "To find a job, I mean."

"Well, you have to give yourself two months," said Meena. "Though I must say we were lucky. We only waited one month."

When it was time to bring out the salad, which was Dimple's contribution to the cooking, she said, "If you don't like it, don't blame me, blame the magazine. I followed the recipe word for word." Everyone stopped talking and watched her set the salad on the coffee table.

"It looks very nice," Bijoy Mullick said. "It looks very American."

Amit would not touch the salad—he said he could not

think of eating crab meat, snails and caviar—but picked the cherries off the top. He said, "Do you know what I'm thinking of just now? I'm thinking of the taste of deep-fried pumpkin flowers."

When the Mullicks had left, Amit said to Jyoti, "That was a damn good job lead. I think I'll follow it up." But to Dimple he said, "I think I impressed Bijoy Mullick this time. The rest is up to God."

Dimple did not answer. She was reading a magazine in bed. In California, she read, people ate vine-ripened tomatoes for breakfast. They also surfed and swam and drove the freeways. She thought she would be very unhappy in California even if the salaries were good out there.

Toward the end of July, Amit began to bathe three times a day. Sometimes he forgot to pull the shower curtains around the bathtub, and the water settled in a pocket between the wall and the tub. Dimple made a point of checking the floor after he came out so she could mop the tiles before anyone found out about the scummy pockets of water. But one evening, when Amit was out getting a half gallon of milk, she saw Jyoti go into the bathroom with a roll of caulk strip in his hand.

"I'm sorry," she said. "I've told him to be careful but . . ." She let the sentence trail off because she felt she was betraying Amit somehow.

"It's vinyl," Jyoti said, "something I helped work on." She thought he was trying not to embarrass her. "It comes in all colors."

Dimple sat on the edge of the tub and held the roll out for him while he bent down on all fours on a lilac bath mat and put caulking strip on two long cracks between the tub and the wall.

"I'm glad you got white," she said. "It's the most

dignified color.'' She didn't mind his softly bulging stomach, and noticed for the first time that he sweated near the small of his back as well as under his arms. She thought it was wrong to notice such things.

"You may like white," he said, "but we spent a fortune marketing it in eight different colors." Dimple thought it fascinating finally to learn, and even hold, what an engineer made. "There—see how easy it is to fix a crack?" he said, taking the roll out of her hand. "Everything quick and clean-cut."

"But will it chip off?"

"No. It's guaranteed not to chip or discolor."

That evening Ina Mullick called, and because Meena was in bed with a bad backache, she talked to Dimple and invited herself over for the next morning. When Dimple told Meena about it, she wanted to get out of bed and bake a cake at once, but Dimple would not let her. Dimple made a coffee cake from a mix, brownies from a recipe she had cut out the week before and a Bengali dessert with Cream of Wheat and lots of raisins and butter. She began to think of it as *her* party for Ina and to hope Meena would stay in bed with a bad backache again.

At a quarter to eleven Ina Mullick rang the doorbell. She was wearing new blue jeans and a pink skinny top and had cut her hair severely short. "I hope you don't mind my inviting myself over like this," she said with a smile, and deposited her large leather purse by the stroller in the hall. "I knew you wouldn't come over if I called you. I mean, I know you wouldn't risk the subway by yourself."

Dimple tried to keep the excitement out of her voice and said, "Shall we sit with Meena in the bedroom? I really don't think she ought to sit up on the sofa."

"Very well," Ina sighed.

Meena and Ina talked of a Miss Singh, more a friend of Ina's than of Meena's, who had just married an American male dancer. Meena was furious.

"But what's wrong with marrying a male dancer?" asked Dimple.

Meena declared the marriage disgusting. "The only male dancer *I* would marry," she said, "would be Uday Shankar. This Miss Singh is marrying just so she can stay in the country."

"But *so what*?" Ina cried. "Miss Singh will never be bed-ridden with backaches thanks to her male dancer. Any Indian girl who comes over alone is entitled to stay on any way she can. Could *you* have come over alone? Could any of us?"

"Even Miss Chakravorty?" asked Dimple.

"Even Miss Chakravorty. She'll have her innocent flirtations and end up marrying some charming young boy from home. Or some perfectly nice American boy from Columbia. It's just like Dimple says—what's wrong with it?"

Dimple started to deny it all; she felt crushed between Ina's approval and Meena's quizzical silence.

When they had exhausted the gossip about Miss Singh and how to make *kala jamun* from pancake mixes, Ina took out leaflets from her large purse and gave them to Dimple and Meena Sen. "I thought you'd like to read them," she said, looking directly at Dimple who smiled weakly and then looked away. Ina said she had picked the leaflets up at a place called Your Mother's Mustache, which was a store where women could sell things they had made, and a place for them to sit down if they wanted to and drink a nickel cup of coffee and add their names to the bulletin board.

"I'd better put the water on for tea," Dimple said. She glanced at a leaflet on the bed near Ina's feet and

saw that someone had written on the top in green felt
pen FREE . . . GIVE ONE TO YOUR FRIEND above the
article's title, "You Don't Need Mr. Clean . . . but Mr.
Clean Sure As Hell Needs You!" and she impulsively
touched Ina's arm and said, "I'm so glad you think of
me as a friend." Ina excused herself to Meena and
followed Dimple to the kitchen.

In the kitchen, over the *halwa*, brownies and coffee
cake, Ina doodled on the margin of a leaflet until there
was a woman with her sari wrapped around her like a
shroud on one side and another woman in a bikini with
a pert bosom on the other. "That's me," she said, with
a shallow laugh. "Before and After. The great moral
and physical change, and all that."

"I'm always a Before," Dimple said. "I guess I've
never been an After."

"I think it's better to stay a Before, if you can," said
Ina Mullick. "Our trouble here is that we imitate badly,
and we preserve things even worse."

"You're not eating," Dimple protested. "You are
such a poor eater!"

Ina sighed. "Why is food our national obsession?
Why don't we make more time for happiness? For
love?"

"I guess it's all that starvation," Dimple said, brushing aside her plate of coffee cake.

After Ina had left, Dimple chained the door very
carefully.

It was not a great job, Amit took pains to explain to
Dimple. A mechanical engineer in heavy boiler maintenance.

"Can you imagine—'Degree preferred but not essential,' " he said bitterly.

Dimple watched the scum thicken on Amit's cold coffee as he talked of fringe benefits and chances of advancement. "Don't worry, you'll get the job," she said. "I pray every night so there's no way you can fail." Then, because the situation demanded an extravagant gesture, she poured herself an extra cup of coffee and asked, "What will you wear? You know you'll have to wow them on the interview day."

Amit had two Barkat Ali suits and decided on the navy blue rather than the pinkish brown. "I can borrow a tie from Jyoti. He's too big; otherwise I could have borrowed his shirt as well."

"I'll fix your tie," she said quickly. "What would you like, the Windsor or the half-Windsor?" She had learned to tie a knot from a brochure she had picked up in a men's clothing store on Park Street where her father had done the dowry shopping. Learning to tie a knot had been her final maidenly accomplishment. She had read and reread the instructions, because in those days of waiting the man in the brochure had been more real to her than Amit. She liked Indian instructions; they were always so explicit. She would invest fierce love into knotting Amit's ties. Her mother had never learned to knot ties. This brochure had devoted sixteen diagrams to tying the Windsor knot.

"I'll do it myself," Amit said. "And remember, wives count for a lot when it comes to hiring and promotion in this country. You might have to meet the bosses."

"I'd better take tips from Ina Mullick."

"No," Amit said firmly. "I think we can learn all that we need to from the Sens."

"Tell me more about the job."

But Amit was secretive. He instructed her not to mention to anyone, not even to the Sens, that he was finally interviewing for the boiler maintenance job, in case it didn't come through. He did not like others to know of, or sympathize with, his failures. She felt it was cruel of him to make her tiny promises of a new life and then withhold the details. If she knew where they would be living, how much salary he expected, she could sit with her *Better Homes and Gardens* and better imagine a nest for herself.

"Can I at least tell my parents that there's a possibility?" But when she looked for aerogrammes in the shoebox in which she kept all stamps and stationery, she found she had run completely out of them.

"I guess your heart's still in Calcutta," Amit said. "You write too often to your parents."

Insomnia was what she feared most. Between two and four in the morning she thought she heard men putting keys in the front door and roaches scuttling in the closet. In those waking nightmares, the men had baby faces and hooded eyes. She lay in bed, afraid to close her eyes and miss the men treading softly on the wall-to-wall carpet, lay in bed with her eyes fixed on the ceiling and the sheet drawn up to her chin. From the next room there was only the warm noise of bodies turning in sleep; she envied them their sleep. She thought of sleeping bodies as corpses. Sometimes when she could not sleep, she slipped out of the humid coffin of her bed, stood quietly by the window and looked down on empty gray streets—in that hour of the morning she thought of streets as badly healed scars on a giant body—let her fingers trail over the windowsill and Venetian blinds and waited for something to happen, waited for a drunk or a hoodlum to distract her from the men with baby faces and the quietly industrious roaches. And this morning she looked at Amit beside

her—he had taken over part of her pillow and the lu-
minous dial of his watch said three-thirty—and because
she could not sleep he seemed unreal to her, like all
sleeping people. She thought if she were to shut her
eyes and listen for fumbling keys at the front door, she
could make Amit die in his sleep. So she stepped out
of her white sheets, testing the rug with her toes to
make sure the floor was where it should be, pulled on
her borrowed bathrobe, walked swiftly across the room
and stood staring at the gray streets until it was time to
go back to bed, lie awake and worry and get up again,
slip her arms through the sleeves of the bathrobe, walk
to the window and let her fingers trace designs on the
dusty window ledge.

There was a noise of water running in the kitchen. It
was not the noise of men fitting keys in locks. This was
precise; water falling on a plate in a kitchen sink. She
buttoned her bathrobe, clutching the loose folds of
quilted cloth at her bosom and pulled the wide collar
up to her chin. Then she raced barefoot on the noiseless
rug to the kitchen's swinging door.

"Sorry," Jyoti apologized from the kitchen. "I was
making a cup of coffee and I spilled water on the floor."
In the harsh light, Jyoti's face was baggy; to Dimple
his eyes seemed hooded.

"Here, let me do it," Dimple said, trembling. "It's
not a man's job to make coffee in the middle of the
night." She bent down and sponged the wet shining
area of the linoleum, aware that her body was bulky in
the bathrobe, aware that Jyoti could not see its taut
curve under the thick quilting. Jyoti took another mug
off a hook from a shelf above the counter and measured
a teaspoon of instant coffee into it, then added two
spoons of sugar. She lifted the kettle from the stove—
it had never felt so heavy—and poured steaming water

into both mugs and stirred the coffee with the same spoon. She thought it was a miracle that she hadn't dropped the kettle and scalded them both.

"How is Meena sleeping?" Dimple asked, but she was thinking how handsome and sincere Jyoti looked in his light blue pajamas with vintage cars printed on them. She tried not to look directly at him—no one had told her how to behave with a husband's friend in pajamas in the middle of the night—but set her gaze on his chest and left shoulder, a safe area, that could not embarrass either of them. "I wish I could sleep soundly." She wished she had wakened Amit and told him where she was going; now it seemed a deliberate betrayal.

"Cream?" Jyoti asked and half rose out of his kitchen chair so that she could see the tops of his pajama bottoms.

"No thank you," she said quickly. "Please sit down. In fact, I shouldn't even be drinking coffee; it'll probably give me worse insomnia." She thought of the one time she and Pixie had drunk coffee in the Skyroom— of course iced coffee was not the same thing; it was too childish—and how frightened she had been of doing the wrong thing. In her Ballygunje dream house she would serve only coffee: tea was so desperately ordinary.

Then he began talking very casually about a murder in Nevada or Nebraska and she thought it was because she would not look at him, because he wanted her to be relaxed, to enjoy the coffee. Talking about murders in America was like talking about the weather, and she was glad that an elderly couple had been fatally shot on a fishing trip so that she did not have to feel guilty about Amit.

"To be shot is bearable, I suppose," Jyoti said. "But

to be dismembered after being shot, that's what really gets me.''

"Before or after," Dimple said gaily, "what does it matter? If you are killed, you are killed. By the way, what time is it?'' She thought that if Amit got the job she would buy a watch—an Omega with hands and numbers that lit up in the dark—and be able to record moments like this.

"They never found the heads!'' Jyoti snickered. "The gunman must have had a macabre fetish.''

"I get so confused here," Dimple said. "Nebraska, Nevada, Ohio, Iowa; they all sound the same to me.''

"Don't worry. If Meena could do it, then you have nothing to worry about.''

She wished she had a prettier robe; how horrible to be dismembered in the faded quilted robe she was wearing.

"You are a lot smarter than Meena. I think you are even smarter than Ina Mullick.''

"Shall I heat the cream for you?'' she asked. "That's one thing the Americans don't know. Coffee or tea tastes much better if you make it with hot milk.''

"I heard that Vinod Khanna offered you a job in his boutique. I don't think you should take it. I mean, he's a very nice guy but I wouldn't want you to work for him, if I were Amit.''

"Why, what does he do? I could be making some money at least.''

"Don't worry about money. Amit will find work.''

"I can take care of myself if he tries any funny business. Anyway, what time is it?'' she asked with forced gaiety.

"Four-fifteen.''

"You should go to sleep so you won't be late for work

tomorrow. I'm glad I don't have to get up early like you.''

Jyoti pushed his chair back and set the half-full mugs in the sink. "I don't want you to wash them now," he said. "That's an order. Meena can do them in the morning when she makes breakfast. She won't mind."

Dimple went back to bed, not to sleep but to reconstruct the scene. In memory, the details were as fragile as the scene itself.

At five Amit sat up in bed and said he was thirsty. When she went into the kitchen—it was still dark in the windowless kitchen and she had to turn on the light—she saw the two dirty mugs in the sink. She washed them quickly, then carried the water to Amit. Some drops spilled on his pillow as he drank. "I'm scared," he whispered. "I'm goddamn scared about the interview tomorrow. You don't know how lucky you are to stay home and do nothing better than looking after a husband."

"Don't worry; you're the best candidate. You just wear Jyoti's tie with your blue suit. You know you're the best."

"You are saying that because you think I want you to say that."

"No, honestly, I'm sure you're the best candidate."

"You are lying to me. You think a wife is supposed to say such things to her husband."

"Okay, okay, have it your way," she sighed, turning her back to him. "You're not the best."

The day after the interview for the job of boiler maintenance engineer, Amit cut his finger trying to change a light bulb in the kitchen.

"You're too impatient," Dimple said. "You should

have waited until Jyoti came home from work. He's used to doing these things.''

''What do you mean?''

She tried to explain that she had not meant that Jyoti could change light bulbs without hurting himself. But Amit would not listen. She was bitter that marriage had betrayed her, had not provided all the glittery things she had imagined, had not brought her cocktails under canopied skies and three A.M. drives to dingy restaurants where they sold divine *kababs* rolled in *roti*. She remembered that Milt Glasser had set her on a counter, fixed a drink and said she was pretty, and that Jyoti had said she was smarter than Ina Mullick, and Ina had said she used to look a lot like Dimple. So many compliments in so short a time; she'd never been complimented in her life before coming to New York because it would have made her egotistical and hard to marry off.

''I know what you're thinking,'' Amit mocked. ''You're thinking you married a bum, a good for nothing.''

''I didn't say that,'' Dimple protested. ''Don't do all the thinking and talking for me.'' But her words were unconvincing, for she believed, though she tried to forget, that a man without a job wasn't a man at all.

Between three and four the next morning Dimple thought of seven ways to commit suicide in Queens. The surest way, she felt, would be to borrow a can of Drāno from under the kitchen sink and drink it, diluted slightly with water. She could see herself as a Before and After type of TV commercial: human face and feet and an S-trap for a body. The least certain, she thought, would be to slip a green garbage bag over her head and tie it with a string around the shoulders. The idea appealed to her sense of beauty: a green world, plastic smooth and soft, until her nostrils trembled and her eyes bulged and a green death overtook her. There was one snag, of course—there was always a snag in dreaming up perfect endings and solutions—she was sure she would not be able to tie the mouth of the garbage bag tightly enough.

In the days of waiting for some word about Amit's job, she clipped five recipes for chicken wings, baked an upside-down pineapple cake, ironed eight cotton saris for herself and Meena, did the laundry all by herself in the basement once and listened to Amit say fifty-one times "I know it will click but why don't they hurry up?" One Sunday Jyoti took Amit, Archana, Dimple and Ina to Jones Beach so Amit would not brood over his interview. Dimple could not remember what the sea and sky and beach looked like, but she did remember feeling envious of Ina. Ina went to the beach in a peasant skirt and smock that she said she had bought in Colaba Causeway, Bombay, but which looked very American on her. Dimple kept seeing herself through Ina's eyes, or rather imagined she was seeing herself through "Ina's eyes, and felt ashamed of her sari-swathed skinny body: it seemed so inappropriate a body for having fun on an American beach. That night she had a new dream: She was walking on the beach. A crowd had gathered just ahead. Something strange has been washed up on the beach. A whale, a porpoise, a shark, she heard people say. She fought her way through a crowd that suddenly disappeared. At her feet lay Ina Mullick, in Dimple's sari, a thin line of water spilling from her mouth.

The job came through on the next to last Wednesday in August. Though Amit kept muttering, "It's not challenging enough,'' Dimple could tell from the way he hummed Tagore songs in his bath that he was happy. *Challenging* seemed to be a recently acquired word for Amit, a replacement for *secure employment*, and Dimple listened for the tone in which it was used to determine if it meant good or bad. She realized that he was full of new words in his conversation: even the Bengali sentences were peppered with American words. Once, when emptying the pockets of his pants, Dimple had come across a scrap of paper with words like *frontier justice*, *crisis management*, *relationship*, *challenging*, *constructive* and *confrontation* listed neatly in columns. She had expected to find addresses, perhaps, a job lead or even a mysterious telephone number. She would have known how to cope with jealousy; it was such a strong, dependable, familiar emotion. How she longed to be positively and absolutely jealous! But she had felt helpless against Amit's list of useful words and phrases.

In the next few days, she could tell from the others' reactions that she had become hard to please. She looked constantly at ads in newspapers for furnished apartments, looked up real estate agents in the Yellow Pages but did not have the nerve actually to call, brought out old copies of *Better Homes and Gardens* from the linen closet and stared for hours at pictures of beds and sofas. The search for a place to live gave her a new kind of certainty, almost an arrogance: she knew she was boring Meena with descriptions of The Breakfast Nook and The Boudoir, but she didn't care. The Sens' living room, especially the blue sofa and the speckled rug, had now become hideous to her. Was it only a few days ago, she thought, she had worried about a beer stain? It was all so shabby, so bare. Life had held out such promises but was so slow to deliver! She wanted big leather chairs with chrome arms and legs and lamps that dominated the room with their enormous curves. When she helped Meena dust and sweep, when she lifted the plastic flowers out of place and dragged the rag over the cabinet or television, she felt like a hypocrite. No one knew how she hated the furniture. Nobody could tell she really wanted to break and smash each piece and squirt dust on the walls. Once, while pretending to dust each petal of the plastic flowers, she managed to twist and break off three petals.

"Oh, I'm terribly sorry," she cried. There were tears in her eyes. "How can I be so clumsy! Do you think we could glue them back together?" She held the pink petals, grotesque and stiff like detached ear lobes, in her cupped palm.

"Don't worry," soothed Meena. "They were very cheap." She promised to buy more and teach Dimple to make Ikebana arrangements with plastic flowers.

"When we get a place in Manhattan, you must make me an Ikebana arrangement, Meena," she said. It was a relief that no one knew how much she hated plastic flowers. When she was about to throw out the torn petals, she felt guilty, as if she had intended to throw out parts of her own body, so she sneaked the three petals to the Sens' bedroom and stored them in the purse where she kept her passport, health certificate and gold jewelry. She thought of the incident as "a narrow escape," though she couldn't be sure from what she had escaped, or how.

The problem of where to live was settled by the Mullicks, who said that Prodosh and Marsha Mookerji were going on sabbatical leave for a semester and would be willing to sublet their university apartment near N.Y.U., but that, as subletting was not strictly legal, the Basus would have to pretend they were Prodosh's cousins.

A week before they were to move to Manhattan, Meena Sen had a daughter and the Basus had to delay their departure so Dimple could look after Archana and help with housework. Jyoti said that Meena had cried uncontrollably in the recovery room when she had been told she had had another daughter.

Part Three

S TARS, Dimple recalled having read somewhere, implode: she felt like a star, collapsing inwardly.

She stood with Amit, shoulders almost touching, and looked out on Bleecker Street from the Mookerjis' window.

"What's wrong?" Amit asked.

"Nothing," Dimple said. "it's such a nice apartment, I'm afraid I might break something or forget to water the plants."

"I wish we had found a place in Queens. You know, on any of the streets off Kissena Boulevard." Amit turned away from the window and tested the dryness of soil in a potted Swedish ivy that was hanging from a basket on the wall.

The high-rise apartment on Bleecker Street was full of closets and mirrors. Marsha had emptied two closets for the Basus; the others were full of silk shirts, wool pants, suitcases with faded labels, hampers, dusty magazines tied together with string, a scorched ironing board. Dimple spent hours going through the closets. Also drawers: she was thrilled when she found a pair of mauve-tinted sunglasses and tried them on in the bathroom. Seeing herself in the mirror above the sink, she thought of astronauts floating in space, their faces invisible behind plastic bubbles.

She wrote her mother that Amit and she had moved into a fantastic apartment belonging to N.Y.U., and that there were two bathrooms and bright orange shower curtains and a floral wastebasket so pretty that she hated to throw trash in it, and a stereo and sixty-two plants (some were very small but she had to water them all) and a red rocking chair that she was afraid to sit on, and a lovely kitchen with shiny wipe-clean counter tops, a French coffee maker and Danish casseroles, and would she please give the new address to Pixie and tell her to write as soon as possible.

She could tell Amit was happy in his job though he kept saying the job was not challenging enough and that he regarded it as a stepping-stone to something better. On their fifth evening in the Mookerjis' apartment, as she watched him make notes on the margin of *The Wall Street Journal*, she said, "The truth is I feel very tired these days. I mean, I don't have the energy to baste the chicken every fifteen minutes, which is what the recipe calls for." Amit said, "It's probably because you eat so little." He did not look up from the paper. So she took the easy way out: she lost her temper, started to cry. She said, "I feel sort of dead inside and all you can do is read the paper and talk to me about food. You never listen; you've never listened to me. You hate me. Don't deny it; I know you do. You hate me because I'm not fat and fair." Then she ran out of the room and picked the oven mitts off the counter as if they were weapons, flung open the door of the oven and lunged forward.

"That smells divine," Amit said, standing just behind her. Standing so close, Dimple thought, that if he were to come any closer he could push her head into the oven and let it warm to 375° and serve it instead of the chicken that was cooking. "I love you; you should know that by now." Then he laughed in a self-conscious way and added, "I love you because you are a great cook. Here, let me lift that out of there."

She let him push her out of his way. He was wearing an extra pair of oven mitts, much fancier than hers, made up to look like bunny faces complete with button noses and calico ears. They made Amit look so absurd that she had to laugh. She was grateful that Marsha kept these weapons to defuse anger.

"There! Nothing to it!" Amit exclaimed, as he set the casserole on the table. "You just like to make a fuss."

"But you forgot the trivet! The table will be scarred!"

The bunny mits hopped into action, rearranging casserole and trivet. Dimple laughed so hard that her shoulders ached and her throat felt full of mucus, as though she had been vomiting.

At the table, as she picked out the best parts of the chicken for Amit, she heard him say, "Boredom is the devil's workshop or however that proverb goes. The point is you must go out, make friends, do something constructive, not stay at home and think about Calcutta."

Dimple recognized *constructive* as one of the words she had seen listed on the scrap of paper, along with all the other new words. She picked absent-mindedly through the wings, neck and back and said, "I'm not brooding about Calcutta. The trouble is, I've stopped brooding about Calcutta.''

"Why don't you take a leg for a change?'' Amit asked. "Do you think American wives always eat wings and necks like you?'' Then he added that she ought to go out more often, make friends with the other women in the building—they had noticed four Indian names on the lobby register—invite them for coffee or go shopping.

"I want you to have the other leg tomorrow,'' Dimple said softly. "Anyway, I love wings.'' She had no idea what American wives did and had no way of finding out. How could she go up to a blond woman in the elevator and ask, peering politely into the Grand Union shopping bag she might be clutching to her bosom, "Excuse me, madam. Do you customarily have legs or wings?'' How could she live in a country where she could not predict these basic patterns, where every other woman was a stranger, where she felt different, ignorant, exposed to ridicule in the elevator?

"If I *could* brood about Calcutta I'd be okay, wouldn't I? I mean, the trouble is I'm not even dreaming about Calcutta anymore.''

"That's a good sign,'' Amit said, smiling. "You're becoming American, but not too American, I hope. I don't want you to be like Mrs. Mullick and wear pants in the house!'' He left the table to get a cold can of beer. He came back with the beer and a wine glass for Dimple, and poured her an inch of foam from his can. "Just this once,'' he begged. "It's a celebration. I mean, we have to celebrate my job and your Americanization, so go on, take a sip of beer.''

"I couldn't,'' she giggled. "It smells awful! You know I'd get sick. You want me to get sick? What's the big idea?'' But she sipped the yellow beer under the foam, sipped delicately, keeping her glass high and her little finger extended outward. The wine glass made her feel knowledgeable, a little like Marsha Mookerji but more like women in commercials.

"Try it, you'll like it, and it's not habit-forming."

"Are you absolutely sure? I won't get drunk?" She sank her lips in the foam. "It's so bitter!"

"You have to get used to it, that's all. But was it true, what you said about Calcutta? I mean, are your dreams *American* now?"

"No, of course not," Dimple said shyly, pushing away her beer. "I was only kidding. I'm a great kidder."

During the day Dimple slept, getting up only to make Amit's breakfast and put his clean clothes out on the bed and listen to his jokes (he had bought a book of jokes and was memorizing them at the rate of five a day). She had given up eating lunch; sometimes if she felt really hungry, so hungry that she couldn't stay in bed, she took leftover rice and curry from the fridge and ate it, without warming it, straight out of the cold Freeze-Tite container. She had given up bathing during the middle of the day, an old Calcutta habit; instead she showered at night, which made her feel different and very modern. Amit had once said, "Why don't you try a sauna? American women are supposed to love saunas. Why don't you be outgoing like them?" But she couldn't see herself sitting naked in a very hot cubicle. Very often, dreams woke her up, but she could not remember what they were about. If it had been Pixie dreaming, Dimple thought, the dreams would have become funny anecdotes to tell others. She wanted to dream of Amit but she knew she would not. Amit did not feed her fantasy life; he was merely the provider of small material comforts. In bitter moments she ranked husband, blender, color TV, cassette tape recorder, stereo, in their order of convenience.

There were no letters from Pixie, just a UNICEF card in mid-September saying, "Hi, Dimple old girl. Greetings from your forgotten friends in good old Cal! Long time no scribble. How come? Here's hoping you'll sharpen your epistolary gifts. Affly, Pixie." She did not get around to answering the card. Every day she thought she should write a letter, something funny and witty with little hints of how American she had become but not so American that she was ridiculous, but every day she kept putting it off. It was too much effort to take an aerogramme out of the big shoebox in the bedroom closet where Amit kept them (he had started to take care of all correspondence in the family), think of funny things she had done or seen and put them in words. The words were never right, she thought, because she had not seen or done anything since coming to the States except sleep and cook. Some mornings, she held her head stiffly on the pillow so she would not be distracted by the pink and lilac flowers on the pillowcase, stared at the ceiling, and tried out beginnings for the eventual letter:

My dear Pixie: How I wish I were in Cal with you. I do miss the hustle and bustle . . .

But *wish* and *miss* were wrong. She was not missing Calcutta really, though it would have been nice to wear new saris and go to the Skyroom and order iced coffee. It was something else, like knowing that if she were to go out the front door, down the elevator (she was frightened by self-service elevators with their red Emergency buttons and wished there were a liftman on a stool to press the right buttons for her), if she were to stand in the lobby and say to the first ten people she saw, "Do you know it's almost October and Durga Pujah is coming?" they would think she was mad. She could not live with people who didn't understand about *Durga Pujah*.

Amit had reminded her many times to write to Pixie. He was very good about thank-you notes and *Bijoya Pronam* letters to relatives. "If you can't write a letter, at least mail her a card from the Humorous Section in Woolworth's," he had advised. She didn't tell him about these imaginary beginnings. She didn't tell him about her immoderate daytime sleeping either. They were unspeakable failings. She thought of them as deformities—sinister, ugly, wicked. She had expected pain when she had come to America, had told herself that pain was part of any new beginning, and in the sweet structures of that new life had allotted pain a special place. But she had not expected her mind to be strained like this, beyond endurance. She had not anticipated inertia, exhaustion, endless indecisiveness. If, in those early days in Queens, the man selling cheesecake had not trapped her, she might have been free, even reckless, might at this very moment have been on her way by taxi to keep trysts with the glittering admen who proffered her tempting pain relievers and foot powder sprays on Marsha's TV set. She would not be in bed in a sunless room worrying herself sick over footsteps in the hall and glass eyes in keyholes. Instead she would be strong and sane.

"What's the matter?" Amit asked after she had put the phone back on its cradle. "I thought you liked talking to Meena."

"Nothing," Dimple said. "She was just telling me about a friend of hers."

"Must have been a sad story."

"The friend died of burns. Meena thinks it was suicide." Setting fire to a sari had been one of the seven types of suicide Dimple had recently devised.

"It could have been an accident. You women are always so melodramatic!"

"It's the first time I've heard Meena cry."

"She just had a baby; what do you expect?"

"What kind of question is that?"

"Okay. Where did she die?"

"Cal, I think. But it could have been in Patna. Her parents lived in Patna."

Dimple hurried into the kitchen and began to chop onions for supper. She didn't want Amit to think she had been crying and she didn't want to answer any questions about Meena's friend whose sari had caught fire when she had been heating milk on a kerosene stove for her three-month-old son. Kerosene stoves were dangerous, but electric ranges could be just as dangerous if you happened to get your head caught in the oven. That was also on Dimple's list. She could not bear the thought of Amit prying the details of the suicide out of her. But why was he ignoring the suicide and reading his newspaper?

"Rule number one," Amit shouted from the living room when she had almost finished with the onion and was starting to chop eight cloves of garlic. "Never wear anything but *cotton* saris while cooking. Synthetic fibers are dangerous."

That night, trapped between the cold wall and Amit's heavy body, in postnightmare lucidity she sought revenge. In sleep the body had lost its compact strength, also its capacity to excite fear in her. She had a sudden desire to examine the body, touch the curves of cheek and chin, trace all dents, depressions, scars, probe the weakened spots until she knew just where to strike or pierce and make him bleed in the dark. Her own intensity shocked her—she had not considered herself susceptible to violence—so she tried to explain it away as unnatural sexual desire. "Love is dread," she whispered loudly to the sleeper.

In the darkness she fitted her round little chin into a slight hollow of flesh on Amit's left shoulder. Gradually, as she pressed the chin dceper in the hollow, applying light, rhythmical pressure, she began to feel that violence was right, even decent. If she were to ram her chin deeper into the hollow, perhaps she could crush the bone that lay directly under, perhaps she could extract from Amit a thrilling surrender. The darkness was unbearably exciting, taut with angry premonitions, promises. Her own body seemed curiously alien to her, filled with hate, malice, an insane desire to hurt, yet weightless, almost airborne. She dug her chin deep into the depression, so deep that he squirmed in sleep. With a viciousness she thought inappropriate to her wifely status, she said, "I'll wear synthetic saris if I want to! I'll wear any goddamn thing I want to, so there!"

Amit grunted, still asleep. He pulled the light, thermal blanket tightly around himself, as if to protect his body against the monsters of a nightmare. His action, abrupt, decisive, uncovered her thighs, calves and toes, making her feel naked and chilly in spite of Marsha's pajamas.

From nine to eleven-thirty Dimple stayed in bed, awake. When it was exactly eleven-thirty by the travel alarm clock on the night table, she got up to make herself a sandwich. The kitchen sink was dirty; there was a grease ring two inches from the bottom and large turmeric stains around the drain. Two coffee mugs, a plate with congealed egg yolk and partly chewed bacon strips and a skillet with waxy bacon drippings cluttered the counter top. It seemed too much trouble to make a sandwich, even a tomato and cucumber sandwich.

She took a shower to forget the sandwich she had not eaten. When she came out of the bathroom the phone was ringing, and it was Ina Mullick.

"Hello," Ina said, and laughed loudly over the phone. "It's me. I was hoping you would call and invite me over. Marsha used to."

Dimple stood, silent and indecisive, in Marsha's blue wraparound bathrobe (Marsha had not said she could use the clothes but Dimple decided that since Marsha would never know there was nothing wrong with trying out a bathrobe or silk shirt). Then she said, "I'd love you to come over. I've been so busy getting unpacked and settled and all that. It's not like Cal, where you have servants to help. I feel I'm going out of my mind with work." If she had set her mind to it, she could have emptied her suitcase and two handbags in about ten minutes. Amit had emptied his bag and put everything neatly in drawers in the first half-hour. He didn't know that she kept everything under the bed; she had to squat down and pull out the suitcase every morning for new panties. It was another of her secrets.

Ina extracted an invitation for coffee at eleven the next day and hung up with a laugh. Dimple wondered why she had allowed herself to be bullied into getting up early. She went back to the kitchen and opened the fridge door and watched the condensation disappear upward. "I must make a cake if Ina comes," she said aloud. Way in the back, behind a six-pack of beer and a plastic pitcher of water, was the casserole dish of leftover mutton curry that she wanted. When she reached for the dish, she almost knocked the pitcher down. "I wonder if we should invite the Mullicks for dinner," she said aloud, and it suddenly occurred to her that she had started to talk to herself, actually talk as if there were another person in the room with her. "And the Sens," she added. There was very little mutton left; it was mostly potatoes and raisins in cold gravy. She remembered that the potatoes were soft, overcooked, because she had been watching TV commercials by the hour. "No, not the Sens. I think we ought to call Milt Glasser." She thought Milt would want to know if his sister's plants were being watered.

The stale curry smelled offensively of garlic. It made her feel trapped, isolated in a high-rise full of Americans who ate hamburgers and pizzas. She thought she might have been a better person, a better wife at any rate, if she could have produced more glamorous leftovers. The time for making decisions was approaching too quickly. A dying bonfire; that was her visual image of life. All these weeks in New York she had done little except devise delays. Now she was running out of tactics, it seemed. She dumped the curry in the sink and ran very hot water over it, watching it disappear.

"If I had eaten that mess," she said, "I would have had to brush my teeth *and* chew gum." Then she gripped the faucet, leaned over the sink and wept.

A half-hour later, to test her powers of survival, Dimple washed her face in cold water, then scoured the sink—she thought there was faint sour odor, like vomit, to leftover mutton curry—sponged the counter tops and the door of the refrigerator, cut a lemon in half and left the two halves in two depressions of the empty egg rack because she had read in a magazine that lemon made refrigerators smell sweet, and went back to bed.

Dear Pixie (ran her imaginary letter):
How are you? Are you still working? Why don't
you try to come to the States and try your luck
with radio and television? It's really (and I'm not
kidding) the land of money, honey and opportu-
nity. Amit wants me to take a course, and I'm
seriously thinking of trying to see if I can do
something at N.Y.U. It'll keep me busy. I wish
you were here, so we could do interesting things
together and go to the movies and have coffee in
little restaurants in Greenwich Village. Can you
believe we've ended up living in ''the Village''—
the very place we heard so many stories about in
Cal? Good old Cal; it's not like N.Y., but it's a
great city . . .

Still not right. It was exasperating, she thought; all
she wanted was to write to her best friend and it came
out absurdly forced and patronizing. Friendship was
impossible through letters. Conveying New York, Ina
Mullick, her nightmares, the ''phase'' (as Amit called
it) she was going through—all impossible to talk about,
let alone describe in English or Bengali. There were no
words she'd ever learned to describe her daily feelings.
She would have to give up trying to write. She would
give up trying to preserve old friendships. Because there
was nothing to describe and nothing to preserve.

The police sirens in the street below woke her. She
hated the shrill wail though she heard it often enough
from this apartment, more often than in Queens. The
air was never free of the sounds of sirens growing
louder, or gradually fading. They were reminders of a
dangerous world (even the hall was dangerous, she
thought, let alone the playground and streets). She had

a gallery of monsters: old alcoholics and young dope fiends asleep in doorways; huge black men in leather jackets and small dark men shouting to her in English she didn't understand or in Spanish; Puerto Rican girls in tight sweaters and pants who looked almost like Indians except that they could mug and stab and kill.

It was three-twenty-three; no use trying to dream after three o'clock in the afternoon. But it was no use getting up either, or brushing her teeth and making coffee and tidying the bed and vacuuming the living-room rug and sweeping away all signs of her secretive life. Amit never came back before six-thirty. She felt very safe.

"What the hell do you do all day?" he asked. "In the next incarnation I want to be a wife and sit at home and do nothing."

"I haven't been doing nothing," Dimple said. "I was planning a dinner for Bijoy and Ina Mullick."

"Let's have the Sens over also," Amit said. He looked surprised and enthusiastic and began speculating on what they should serve.

"I thought we could invite that boy, what was his name, Milt or something like that. I thought we could invite him with the others."

"Why him? I don't have anything to say to him."

"It doesn't look nice if we ignore him. After all, we're staying in his sister's apartment," Dimple persisted.

"Thursday, around eight?" Amit asked, and before she had nodded her agreement, he dialed the Mullicks' number.

Milt Glasser was the first to arrive. She was on her way from the kitchen to the bathroom to comb her hair—she had been deep-frying onion rings to garnish the *pilau* and knew that bending over the steam had made the hair on her crown curl—when Milt rang the doorbell and came in with his own key. Dimple was momentarily frozen, wanting to scream, when she heard the scratching at the door and then saw it move. He carried two bottles of Liebfraumilch.

She held out her right hand to shake because she had practiced the handshake and "I am so glad you could come, I hope the curry will not be too hot for you, I made it only medium-hot with you in mind, and you must see the plants, they are flourishing (she was proud of that word) by the window." But Milt entered so swiftly, twisting his long elastic body and bending over her head (over the unpleasant curls of the crown), kissing her on the right cheek and saying "Hi, Dimple" so softly, that she couldn't say a word.

After that, the evening fell apart for Dimple. She could not remember a whole sequence of actions. If she had been asked to describe the dinner at her home that evening, what the guests had worn or said to each other or how many cans of beer they had consumed, she could not have done it. She heard Ina Mullick tell Meena Sen, "Why don't you put the baby in an empty drawer? I think that's much safer than the bed or the floor. Don't you, Dimple?" And she realized that she must have agreed because she was furiously emptying one of Marsha Mookerji's drawers and, like a nightmare, boxes kept opening, powders spilling; it seemed she was emptying more things than anyone in a lifetime had a right to own, while Meena stood over her with the baby. In the center of the bed there was an untidy pile of printed shirts, patent leather belts, panties and bras (those light, lacy bras that Dimple had been wanting to try on, waiting only for a day when she felt she deserved it, or needed it). Then she carried the empty drawer into the living room and set it on a white shaggy rug on the floor.

"That rug's dangerous," Milt said with a laugh. "It's full of needles and pins. Marsha says she drops them deliberately because she can't stand Popo going barefoot in the house." It had seemed such a curious bit of information about the Mookerjis that Dimple hadn't known what to think of them after that. Were there other booby traps that they each set the other, frightfully brilliant traps that she would probably miss and hurt herself? At one point in the evening all three women were in the kitchen, though Dimple could not think later what they had been doing in that tiny room or how they had fitted in without bumping hips and breasts. Dimple still thought of Meena Sen as enormously pregnant; the new Meena, tall and flabby, did not really exist. She liked kitchens, considered them ideal places for confidences. She could have spent the entire evening surrounded by canned soups, cereal boxes, glass jars of rice and pulses—the pillars of security—thinking of Milt's kiss. A kiss was never a happy event. But Ina led them out too soon.

"Don't *you* think she looks like the mother rather than the father?" Ina asked Milt and Dimple.

"Yes," Dimple said, but she was thinking not of the velvet-faced infant in Marsha's drawer, now back in the bedroom, but of broken taps on Dr. Sarat Banerjee Road, of vomiting until her eyes were bulging yellow and red-veined, of chasing bleeding rodents.

"You must decide on a name quickly," Ina urged. "To go nameless in New York is a terrible fate. That baby doesn't deserve that. She's going to have enough problems anyway."

"We are waiting for a letter from Jyoti's mother," said Meena. "I want Sushmita but Jyoti thinks his mother will want Alokananda. I think that's such a horrible, old-fashioned name.''

"Look," said Milt Glasser, "since she's an American kid, why don't you give her a good all-American name? Judy or Susan or something.''

"*Eesh*, terrible," said Meena. "I couldn't even talk to my own daughter if her name was something like Judy. I wouldn't know what to say to her.''

"And everyone would take her for a bloody Anglo or a Christian when she went back home," said Jyoti.

"But New York's home, for chrissakes!" Milt protested. "Okay, another suggestion. What about Bella? Definitely not Christian and, who knows, she might be the first woman president of the United States.''

"But I don't want her to be president, poor thing. I want her to marry a nice Bengali engineer like her daddy," Meena Sen said.

The infant began to cry in the next room. "She knows we are discussing her fate," Dimple said. "She wants to join in so she isn't stuck with anything she doesn't like.''

Everyone laughed. Dimple and Meena left the room to see what was wrong. When they came back, Dimple carrying the baby awkwardly against her hip and Meena holding the empty drawer, the problems of naming Bengali baby girls in New York were still being explored.

"How about naming her after a film star like Jaya or Sharmila?" Ina was asking.

"Well, if it's got to be a film star," Jyoti said, "it has to be Marilyn Monroe or nothing.''

"How about Alice?" Milt asked, walking up to Dimple and fondling the infant. His fingers were huge against its face. He was probably one of those Americans who were good with children. They all seemed to know exactly what to say or do without seeming unmanly. Amit would never touch or hold an infant. She thought she had never seen fingers as huge as Milt's. "How about Alice Cooper Sen? Hey, wait a minute! She has a dimple, just like you!"

"So what?" Dimple exploded. "So what if she does? Don't you dare suggest Dimple as a name!"

"Where?" Meena asked harshly, putting down the drawer and taking the child out of Dimple's arms to examine its tiny cheeks for little depressions and dents. "Do you mean this thing here?" She pointed at a faint crease near the mouth. "It's pretty. It's not a deformity, you know."

"Who said it was a deformity? I like dimples, for God's sake!" Milt exclaimed, smiling wickedly at Dimple.

"It's time for dinner," she retorted.

At dinner Amit told a joke about what one man was saying to another man but Dimple did not catch what either man was saying because she was running between kitchen and dining area with casserole dishes and the two bottles of wine. If necessary, she could always look it up in Amit's joke book. He said he had only twenty-five more jokes to memorize in the book he had bought on the day they moved away from Queens. She thought that if she had any money of her own she would buy him a new joke book and it was terribly unfair of him not to give her any money. Since they went to the Grand Union together every Saturday, there was no way for her to cheat from the weekly shopping either. Between the coconut-shrimp curry and the dessert, she told a funny story about what Pixie had said to the tangerine man in Gariahat Market last winter. Pixie had bought a dozen tangerines and the tangerine man had promised that they would be sweet as sugar or he would refund double her money. But Pixie had come back to the tangerine man the next day and said that the tangerines might be like sugar, but that she liked her tangerines to be as sweet as *gur* and would he therefore shell out the money he had promised. Dimple was quite pleased with herself; even Bijoy, who'd been quiet all evening, giggled in his high-pitched voice. They all took turns telling it in English for the benefit of Milt, but there was no English equivalent for *gur*. Dimple could see it was going to turn out badly, like one of Amit's jokes.

She thought of Pixie. Pixie was full of success stories. Pixie had written recently to say that she was bored by broadcasting and was now trying her luck as a fashion designer for a boutique in Ballygunje bank-rolled by one of her new friends. Everyone seemed to want more Pixie stories, so she tried telling one or two more, in English from the beginning, especially the one about Pixie's trying to interview a lady gynecologist who started to get too explicit, but they were not as effective as the one about the tangerines. She felt she had betrayed Pixie because the one consistent thing about Pixie was that she was funny.

"You should lay the baby down on her stomach," Ina Mullick said. "I know all about it because I have no babies."

Meena Sen scooped the baby out of Marsha's drawer and burped it against her shoulder. The baby's face was like a raisin. The face lay against a white towel (it was printed all over with roses) that Dimple had given Meena so Meena could burp the baby. The baby made a strange noise and yellowish liquid spurted out, covering a pink rose. Dimple thought babies were funny little creatures but they had no right to mess up a pretty towel by burping and vomiting.

Dimple did not drink any of the Liebfraumilch. If

Amit had not been there she thought she might have permitted herself a sip or two. But Amit would always be there beside her in his shiny, ill-fitting suits, acting as her conscience and common sense. It was sad, she thought, how marriage cut off glittering alternatives. If fate had assigned her not Amit but some other engineer, she might have been a very different kind of person.

At the door, when she saw Milt Glasser getting ready to leave and monkeying around with Ina Mullick, Dimple wondered if he were about to give her a good-night kiss. But because she was ready, because her body was taut and expectant, her cheek held up politely so that a tall man would not have too hard a time stooping, there were no good-night kisses.

She slept very soundly the next morning and Amit was almost late for work because he had to start breakfast for himself. Dimple slept all through the early afternoon also, getting up only once to eat leftover shrimp curry with a slice of white bread. At 4:09 P.M. she woke up and realized that she was hungry again. Since the bread had not been put away—she had been too tired— but was still out on the counter lying on its side, looking vaguely mutilated by the bread knife which was also still on the counter beside the bread, she cut herself a second slice. Just as she was about to bite into it, she noticed a small cluster of mold in the bottom left corner. She studied the mold, holding open the door of the refrigerator for more light, marveling at the greenish blue color and soft texture. It was shaped like a flower, she thought. Using her fingernails as knife points, she tore the mold-flower out of the slice and threw the rest of the bread away. She wished she had simply bitten into the slice with her eyes shut. There were too many images of corrosion within the apartment. Noticing them probably signaled the beginning of something bad. There would be other signs if she gave in now. Like telling people her dreams and trying to pass them off as jokes. Then urging people, between nervous giggles, to guess the *real* meaning of her dreams, until they backed away, apologetic, embarrassed. Then dreaming dreams that they told her were typical. She poured herself a bowl of Wheaties and skim milk and sat down formally at the dining table. She would not discuss her dreams with anyone. One must draw the line somewhere; one must stand on principle. After the fifth spoonful, she realized she was not hungry, was, on the contrary, feeling ill and had spilled milk and cereal flakes on her clothes. There was nothing to do except go back to bed and let the soggy flakes harden and stain Marsha's blue zip-up robe.

She had not expected to sleep, only to lie in bed, the sheet pulled up to her dimpled chin, listening for footsteps in the hall. Silence disturbed her. When she could detect no thumps and knocks on the door, no dangerous shuffling of drunkards, no keys being slid into locks, only a vast, unnerving silence, she began to panic. In a mirror across the room, she saw herself, a small, stiff lump, hair arranged like black bat wings against the sky blue pillow. Catch a fatal disease, she told herself. Of all fatal diseases, leukemia was the most glamorous.

That night, after Amit cut his finger, she said, ''You do believe me, don't you? I swear it wasn't my fault,'' as she got the Band-Aids out of the bathroom cabinet.

Amit sat on a white leather ottoman, knees bent, calves tensed. Dimple was struck by the air of unaccustomed theatricality around him. He seemed a little like a comic character actor in a Bombay movie as he held out his bleeding index finger and thumb toward her.

"All I wanted was romance," Amit said with a nervous giggle, "and look what happened to me."

Her hands described tiny circles of helplessness, then burrowed as if for refuge in the folds of her cotton sari. "I didn't realize it was you sneaking up from behind like that," she said. "I thought it was someone evil; you know what I mean? Some burglar who had broken in through the living-room windows." She tried not to look at the starlike drop of blood on his shirtfront.

"How could anyone come in through the window?" Amit laughed. "We're on the fourteenth floor, for God's sake!"

"In America, anything is possible," she retorted. "You can be raped and killed on any floor."

She fumbled with the Band-Aids, not sure how to center the strips on the cuts.

"There's no virtue in being so overcautious," Amit said. "You see what happens then?" He pushed his injured hand close against her face. She drew back, but not before she had noticed the faint red streaks dyeing the wrinkles of his fingertips.

"But I didn't know it was you!" she cried, squeezing too much antiseptic cream on Amit's thumb. "How could I have known it was you? You never come up from behind like that! I just grabbed whatever was handy and gouged with my eyes shut."

"So much for romance!" Amit said.

She thought it best to let him exhaust his bitterness in small exclamations. He had a right to be bitter. He had come home late from work (later than usual so that she had been more nervous than usual, her head full of half-remembered reports of breaking and entering, of alarming coughs in the hall and police sirens in the streets) and perhaps to make up for his lateness he had pretended sexual desire, creeping up on her from behind as she was chopping garlic, and she had lunged at him with the tiny paring knife. The action passed through her mind like an instant replay on TV but the replay explained nothing. Perhaps grabbing the knife—the handle had been sticky with garlic juice—had been tactlessly instinctive, she told herself. Or perhaps she was capable of unimagined, calculating violence. It would remain a mystery.

"Come into the bathroom," she said. "Let me fix your finger nicely."

"You mean, this time you want to chop it off altogether?" But he followed her into the bathroom, and stood at attention on the purple Kodel mat.

"You're too tall that way," she objected. "I'm afraid you'll have to sit." She indicated the edge of the bathtub, which was spotted with hair and dried, gray soap bubbles.

Amit pulled down the Kodel-covered lid of the toilet seat and lowered himself on it heavily. "Okay, boss," he said.

Behind his head, in the open medicine cabinet, were deep rows of bottles, jars, tubes, testimony to her acquisitiveness. She stared for a long time at the cabinet as if seeking among its contents some clue to her life, some foreshadowing of change. In a trance, she raised her right knee and rested it delicately on the Kodel-furry edge of the toilet lid, then reached for something on the highest shelf, allowing the smooth taut skin of her bare midriff to touch the right side of her husband's head. Her fingers moved in a downward spiral among vitamin pills and headache tablets, spray deodorants for him and roll-ons for her, eyeshadows in discreet plastic cases, pillars of dental floss, Q-Tips, hairbrushes and

brutal injector blades, then stopped briefly at a pretty
can of vaginal spray that she had bought with a collec-
tor's pride in an uncrowded hour at the supermarket and
that made her feel more sophisticated, more modern
than all her Calcutta friends, and finally the fingers
halted on the top of Amit's head. The night might be
salvageable after all.

"Well, Florence Nightingale, how about it?" Amit
asked. "What do you have to offer?"

Something in the momentary physical arrangement,
injured husband squatting on the toilet while his wife
ministered to him with exquisite grace, conspired to
destroy heroic proportions, she thought. Her mind,
flooded with irreverence, tried to step back from the
edge, to seize some muddy cliché so that it would not
be washed away, to ponder the domestic virtues of duty
and docility until the nasty passions subsided.

"What a horribly deep cut!" she exclaimed.

Amit rotated his injured hand so that she could examine the cut in better light. His action had a reverse
effect on Dimple. She thought of that hand, especially
the large beige palm, as a canvas for future designs.
Her own ruthlessness appalled her. Perhaps she was
one of those people she had read of in translated English novels of the last century, people incapable of love.
She pretended great sorrow. How awful to be hurt, to
bleed in the bathroom and wait for a wife to erase the
pain! But his very defenselessness thrilled her, revived
her memories of other bathrooms, where shelves had
been lined with yellowing newspaper and where ants
had hung like moving ropes on damp, dark floors,
where roaches had scurried in and out of rusty drains,
and where, once, a mouse with a battered head had cast
her a look of utter contempt just before its death.

"I was just protecting myself," she said. "You do understand that, don't you?"

"Okay, okay," Amit answered, grabbing the Band-Aids from her and laying them neatly over his cuts. "At least that lets me out of dishwashing."

"But you never do the dishes anyway!"

"So what?"

"This wouldn't have happened if we had stayed in Calcutta," Dimple whispered. "I was never so nervous back home. Do you think I was nervous?"

"I don't think I ever knew you in Calcutta," he said.

By the end of the week she had stopped talking to him except to issue curt information like "Dinner's on the table," or "Your clean undershirt's on the bed." In the evenings he read his newspaper or watched television while she made a great show of reading an old copy of *Femina* that Meena Sen had given her, or a pink brochure called the "Khanna Cultural Society Information Bulletin," which Vinod Khanna had mailed to Amit with a special note to her: "The offer of a job is still open. Pl. call if you want to help edit the bulletin, my maiden voyage."

There were useful things to learn from the Khanna bulletin:

SPECIAL OFFER: ALL MEMBERS OF THE KCS BUYING THEIR ROUND-TRIP TICKETS FROM US WILL RECEIVE AS FREE GIFT AN ELECTRICAL APPLIANCE (220 OR 110) OF CLIENT'S CHOICE UP TO MAXIMUM VALUE OF $20 (RS 170!). FOR INFO. CALL KIRAN MEHRA.

ARE YOU DREAMING OF YOUR FUTURE? COLLEGE FOR LITTLE ASHOK AND MARRIAGE RECEPTION FOR

DEVIKA? THEN CALL V. KHANNA AND FIND OUT
HIS INSURANCE PLANS FOR YOU!

WANTED: FOR EXTREMELY WELL-BEHAVED IN
MANNERS AND WELL-EDUCATED M.S. IN MECHAN-
ICAL ENGINEERING FROM REPUTABLE UNIVERSITY,
PUNJABI BOY, 27, WHEATISH COMPLEXIONED AND
TALL, A PRETTY, FAIR, TALL PUNJABI-SPEAKING
BRIDE FROM HIGHLY CULTURED BACKGROUND.
BOY'S UNCLE OWNS HOME IN NEW JERSEY.

FILMS AVAILABLE ON REQUEST FOR SCREENING BY
CULTURAL ORGANIZATIONS AND AT PARTIES. ALSO
ALL LATEST HINDI SOUNDTRACKS, TAPES, ETC. FOR
INFO CONTACT V. KHANNA

"How can you read the same thing over and over
again?" Amit asked during a commercial. And because
she was distracted by the TV commercial—it was about
a young wife who had returned to the basics and used
only soap made out of natural products—he was able to
snatch the pink brochure out of her hands.

"Just listen to this," he said and began to read from
Vinod Khanna's brochure. " 'Wanted for a divorced
lady gynecologist of respectable and well-connected
family, a suitable groom. Caste no bar. Lady who has
been settled in U.S. for last nine years, has small female baby. Only persons with refined feelings and serious intentions need apply.' That Khanna fellow is
really too much! He's trying to marry off divorcées!"

"If we bought our tickets now," Dimple said softly,
"we could get a free gift."

"I don't want a free gift."

"How can you be so heartless? Don't you want to

see your mother and Pintu? What about your sister?
Don't I want to see my mother and father?''

"We can't afford it!" He returned to the game on
television. "Besides, we've only been away four
months. What's the matter with you?''

"What would you ask for?" she persisted. "I
wouldn't mind a portable mixer or a clock-radio.''

"I don't want to talk about it, okay?" he said, without taking his eyes off the screen. "I couldn't get leave.
Anyway, I wouldn't even dare ask for leave at this stage,
so don't get your hopes up.''

"I think a mixer would be very nice.''

"You are out of your mind,'' Amit answered.

Ina Mullick dropped in without calling at eleven-
thirty one morning. She sat effortlessly on Dimple's
unmade bed and said that her life was falling apart.
Dimple, unaccustomed to the role of comforting angel,
brought out a stack of old *Feminas* and *Eve's Weeklys*
from under the bed in the hope of sharing with seasoned
columnists this unexpected burden of giving advice.

"No!" cried Ina. "I don't want to look at magazines
now. Can't you see I'm unhappy?''

Dimple, fearing that Ina's unhappiness was conta-
gious, sought protection in a *Femina* picked at random
from the lint-covered stack. A gaudy picture of mutton
vindaloo stood between Ina and herself.

"Hey, didn't you hear what I said?''

"Yes,'' Dimple answered. "You are unhappy.''

"No!" Ina cried. "I mean, this is the real thing. I
don't know why I'm telling you all this when I've got
my own women's group, but I'm twenty-eight years old,
I have an M.Sc. in physics from Calcutta University
and I'm bitterly unhappy.'' She made a curious gesture

with her hands as if she were laying her unhappiness, a limp, cat-shaped creature, on the unmade bed.

"I'm sorry," Dimple said in a sick-room whisper, "I'm so sorry." She would have preferred to stay silent, but the consciousness of being a ministering angel to someone as dramatic and forceful as Ina Mullick goaded her to speech. "Would you like a cup of tea?"

"Stop being so goddamn polite! Stop being so sorry for me. I want to be honest with you, Dimple. Why can't we be honest?" Her voice was very low, an impersonation of reasonableness. "Why can't we be friends?"

Dimple remembered Miss Problem-Walla, but the memory brought her no comfort or enlightenment. The verities of life that came so easily to Miss Problem-Walla and to every other adult in India that she had ever known had been withheld.

"I used to be just like you. It's really amazing, you know," Ina said in an unpleasantly high voice. "I used to be like that with Biju. I'm sure you know what I mean; very evasive and all that. And drank a lot of tea. But no more, I'm telling you. Fini. Period." Her frail bosom rose and fell in rebellious agony, making the huge satin rose on her T-shirt bloom and wilt hypnotically. Dimple thought she looked sickly and too intense, in that T-shirt and those faded blue jeans.

"What women's group do you mean? Are there any Bengalis?"

"God, no! Dimple, sometimes I want to shake you. There are no Bengalis in my group. There are no Meena Sens, no Dimple Basus, no Indians—"

"—I just thought perhaps it would make things easier," Dimple quickly interjected. "I mean, a Bengali would understand your feelings better, wouldn't she?" She went into the kitchen, Ina following, to put water on to boil. Then they retired to the dining room. Dimple had not baked a cake in the past three days; she prayed that Ina would not want some.

Outside, beyond the dark brown heavy drapes, were street sounds, abused brakes and ambulance sirens. Inside, the friendship ran its uncertain course, pleasing nobody. Fear seized the younger woman. If what Ina had said was true, that they were very much alike, then in a few years she too could expect to wear a T-shirt and blue jeans and sit on an unmade bed and tell an immigrant wife her pitiful story.

Ina, sensing a challenge, said, "No one—no Bengali, not my husband, not you, absolutely no one understands me. Do you know that last night I thought seriously of suicide? Now do you get it?"

"How?" Dimple asked, keeping her voice as even, unembarrassed and guiltless as she could.

"Sleeping pills," Ina said.

"I know, but what kind?"

"That's what I like about you, Dimple, you know? Talking to you is like talking to a . . ." Ina sputtered for a moment, "a porpoise! I can't tell if I'm boring you with my human stupidity—or if I'm talking to a fish."

Dimple was grateful when the kettle whistled faintly, allowing her to hide in the kitchen and regroup her forces. The air in the windowless kitchen was warm and humid; the steaming kettle had left condensation tracks on the wall nearest the stove. She thought how lucky she was to be alone among Marsha's appliances, to explore the wonders of modern American living, unencumbered by philosophical questions about happiness.

"I like porpoises," Dimple shouted from the kitchen. "They're so nearly human, aren't they?" She had seen only one in her life, and that too on television, flipping and squealing in a kidney-shaped swimming pool in a suburban backyard while it waited to be freighted clear across the country. A porpoise was an immense, soft, vulnerable creature. At the back of her mind floated a disturbing image of herself as a child, with scarred knees and a pink taffeta bow on her head. When Ina spoke in English, her words were predatory, Dimple realized.

Ina, entering the kitchen noisily, said, "I don't think I'll stay for tea. You're not being supportive. This relationship is going nowhere. Any fool can see that."

Dimple nodded assent, and put the second teacup and tea bag away.

Ina and Dimple did not refer to that incident again. Perhaps Ina concluded that her confession had been premature.

Sometimes she brought little presents—paperbacks, imported cheese, soya bread. Dimple liked the bread and cheese. The books, which were often about middle-aged women committing adultery on their own premises, had nothing to offer Dimple and were returned with only the first chapters and the last pages read.

"Why don't you give her a key?" Amit said bitterly one morning after Ina had kept Dimple on the phone for twenty-five minutes, forcing him to get his own breakfast so he would not be late for work. He hated Ina Mullick.

During their quarrels, he came back again and again to the party at which Ina had dumped the Sens' infant in a wooden drawer as if it had been a lifeless doll, and Ina's friend, Milt Glasser ("some funny business there, too"), had brought wine.

"How could a good woman throw a baby in a box?" he asked.

"She was using common sense. The drawer was the safest place."

He traced Dimple's faults, especially her hints of obstinacy, to her new friendship with Ina Mullick. "You saw what she just did. Kept you on the phone so I would have to fix my own breakfast. She's testing me."

In Dimple's mind, Amit's criticism invested Ina with the glamour of martyrdom. Though she generally flinched from quarrels, she decided not to let him go this time. She said, "What rubbish. She's only trying to be helpful."

"I will listen to no more. Her kind brings nothing but trouble."

Dimple couldn't shut up; she couldn't resist. "She says I should go to work for Vinod Khanna."

"Do not mention his name to me so early in the morning!" Amit exploded, resorting to English to express the full magnitude of his passion. "He is a reprehensible person!" He said all Punjabis were lecherous, dirty and uncultured, especially when they drank, and they drank all the time. Nothing would please them more than to get an innocent and pretty Bengali girl in their clutches.

"You are making it up," Dimple grumbled.

But Amit said, "My dear girl, some of us have more important things to do than make up stories about worthless people."

"Do you think I'm pretty, then?" she asked.

"It's a known fact that Bengali girls are the prettiest girls in India. That is what I meant."

When Ina Mullick came over around eleven-thirty, Dimple allowed herself to be talked into going out for a pizza and a walk. It was a cool day in late October, and Dimple was glad to have one of Marsha's very short jackets to wear. On her, it didn't look short at all. Ina led the way to a little restaurant on Bleecker Street. There were two men eating pepperoni pizza by the slice at the stand-up counter, but the tables were empty.

Ina was in the mood for autobiography. She hadn't been able to discuss it in her women's group. "You see!" Dimple gloated, but Ina ignored her. She said she had led a perfectly useless childhood, just like everyone she knew; she had lived with her parents and older sister in a large, dark apartment in Queen's Mansion on Park Street, eaten too many cakes and ice creams at Flury's and had been a pudgy book-borrower, mostly of Georgette Heyer novels, from the Oxford Lending Library across the street. She had never paid a fine, and that was the proudest accomplishment of her first sixteen years. ("I mean how can I say *that* to my women's group?" she snarled, biting into the pizza and letting the cheese ooze back between her teeth.) She'd taken sitar lessons from an *ustad* until he'd made a pass ("God, we always *said* he'd made a pass. It was the most horrifying thing that had ever happened. But when I think about it now, all he did was to trail his fingers on *didi*'s hand a little longer than was strictly necessary. I feel like an idiot admitting all this!"). He'd been gotten rid of. "And that's it," she said. "I wanted to be a physicist. I wanted to use words like *thermodynamics* and *superconductivity* at parties. And one day when I was ready to start my doctorate, my father announced that I could throw away my books and start packing my bags because he'd found a perfect match for me in America with a suave *rupee*-millionaire. It wasn't even Biju's picture they showed me! Can you imagine!"

"But look how well you've done," Dimple began, trying to bite discreetly so the tomato sauce would not dribble down her chin and stain Marsha's jacket, and the hot cheese would not settle behind her front teeth and burn her. Pizza-eating was always so perilous; she usually came out of it scarred for days.

"Please, just stop it," Ina demanded. "You're avoiding the issue. Can you honestly say I'm doing well when I tell you I'm desperately unhappy? Can't you see that there's a slight contradiction there?"

They did not talk anymore until the pizza had been finished. Then Dimple gathered her scarf and purse and tried to work out her share of the bill. It would have been easier with separate checks, though she found it hard to work out how much tip she should leave on the table. Of course, you couldn't put one medium pizza on two separate checks. "I've got to get going," she said uncertainly. "Amit told me to look for a Grundig TK-244. Or was it TK-600? They're tape recorders, you know."

"Fascinating. And while you're at it, why not look at a Sony cassette C-410 and a Panasonic Deluxe Oven Toaster T93F and a GE color TV XCM719? How dare you worry about crap like that when I'm laying my life bare for you?"

Dimple carried the crumpled check in her left hand and paid for the pizza, the wine and two bottles of Coke and took Ina home with her.

Only one memorable event occurred when Dimple and Ina were returning to the apartment. A young man in a navy windbreaker, carrying a heavy Grand Union bag—Dimple noticed that celery leaves nearly covered his mouth—winked at them in the elevator. It was a slow, deliberate wink, and could not be construed as an accident or a tic. Dimple ignored it—she looked at the wilted leaves instead—but she heard Ina giggle very loudly and was almost certain that Ina had winked back at the young man. Back in the apartment, Ina turned on the television before taking off her trench coat, then flopped on the shaggy white rug and leaned back against the brown corduroy sofa that Dimple felt could easily seat, or maybe sleep, eight people. "I'm not drunk, you understand," Ina said. "I have a low alcohol tolerance, but I am not drunk."

"I didn't say you were. I didn't say anything at all. Did you hear me say anything about anyone in this room being drunk?"

"Just because some guy in the elevator winks at me doesn't mean there's something wrong. I want you to know that, Dimple." Then she added, "What's wrong with me never shows; that's one of my problems."

Dimple tried to assure her that it was perfectly normal for a man in an elevator to wink at other occupants. Especially if he was carrying a heavy load. Heavy weight did something to the muscles and nerves, and produced winks, tics and assorted disorders. She said she had read that in a magazine article not long before.

There was an early-afternoon talk show on TV, one that tried to interest the New York housewife who was too sophisticated for the other afternoon shows. Dimple found herself, over the months, liking both types equally. Today, four fat young men with suety shoulders and long hair tied in ponytails were talking excitedly to the middle-aged interviewer. He wore a dark blazer with shiny buttons. The creases in his pants seemed almost painted on, and even his sideburns were stiff and slimy. His eyes were big, bulbous and fishlike. The young men were called The Four Electric Cows.

THEY SAID:
    We love words. We break them up, hammer
    them down, chisel and pare and make them

new. We love language, we think language, we feel language, we write language, and we say language.

We are volcanoes, we erupt with emotion, erupt with emotion and into language. Eruptions of words, molten lava of words, then we become silent, until we erupt again. We are the medium, the gasoline for the car, the hair for the hair curler, the film for the camera.

INTERVIEWER:
Could you say a poem for us?

THE COWS:
You and
no affirming I
say you
hate no affirming
I hate but yes
denying you
hate I yes
denying affirming
hating
youing and Iing
affirming hating

INTERVIEWER:
Yes, I see. Very nice. But why the noise in the background? It sounds like crickets.

ONE COW:
Right, man. It's a nasal accompaniment. It sets the mood, the added dimension, it sharpens the explosion of feeling and meaning. It says feeling *is* meaning.

INTERVIEWER:
Would you say your work straddles an area between poetry and music?

ANOTHER COW:
Yes, we're singers and seers and poem-sayers
and milkers of language and givers of language
(which is why we call ourselves the Cows, because we give so much). Like a new one we
said on the way down here:

Silly skinny cock
In a silly skinny coop
With a silly skinny claw . . .

Dimple lay on the sofa with a cushion under her head.
"It's not like any Tagore poems or Hemanta Kumar is
it?" She asked wistfully. "Do you remember that old
Hemanta song: 'When the bug of whimsy flutters, and
breaks down your house of cards in your head,' etcetera? I can't remember the rest. I can't seem to remember anything these days."

But Ina had fallen asleep, sitting up. The collar of
her yellow turtleneck hung limp around her slender
throat. Dimple hoped she'd wake up before five-thirty,
have her cup of tea and go home before Amit came back
from work.

In early November Mrs. Dasgupta wrote that Pixie
had married a fifty-three-year-old actor and was hon-
eymooning at the Oberoi Sheraton Hotel in Nariman
Point, Bombay. Mrs. Dasgupta wrote once every two
weeks, filling one side of the aerogramme in her careful, childish handwriting. Dimple could tell by reading

the first sentence what the rest of the letter would usually say because Mrs. Dasgupta was not given to new ideas and was not receptive to news events. She normally wrote: We are all fine, I hope you are both fine, your grandmother's health is as poor as always, she is now counting the days to the end, which is best in the long run because she is in great pain and says she can hear her own bones crumbling. Your aunt Khuku's polyps are worse but she is afraid of hospitals and operations as you probably remember, so they keep growing and growing. Your father's blood pressure is high again and I have told him to take things easy but who am I that he will listen to my advice, he thinks his office is his home and lives in it night and day. You wrote that you have felt weak and tired lately, also light-headed. How are you now? Check with the doctor immediately, they have very good doctors in America, probably the best, so do not delay. Your mother may be an uneducated woman, but she is warning you it could be low blood pressure, anemia, pregnancy or worse. The weather here is turning quite pleasant, the days warm and the nights cool, in fact we have to use a shawl in the evenings, how is the weather there? Accept our blessings, we pray for you every day.

But this time Mrs. Dasgupta had begun the letter without the prescribed questions about Amit's and Dimple's health. She had written: You will be shocked to hear what your friend Pixie has been up to lately. I knew things would end badly when she took that job at the radio station. Now she has managed to get her picture into magazines like *Star and Style* and *Stardust* and anyone can read about her romance and exploits. That's right, she has married a film star, and an ugly one like Prosanto Bagchi at that! The magazines say he is forty-three which means he is probably fifty-three or more and what Pixie sees in him only Pixie knows. As you can imagine her parents are heartbroken—she's brought home a son-in-law who's older than her father! I say it's all their fault for letting her take a job like that, because that's how she met him—doing a silly interview for the radio. He whisked her off to Bombay after a secret ceremony at his sister's place, and all Pixie could do was send a letter to her mother saying that she was sitting by the pool at the Oberoi Sheraton and having a tomato cocktail. I suppose I'll have to give her a present since her mother gave you that rhinoceros-shaped ashtray, but I told your father I'm not going to give her anything until she comes to our house and introduces her husband to us. It's a matter of common politeness. If we do not stand on some ceremony, we might as well go back to the dark ages. I hope you still pray every day and aren't picking up any bad habits from all those influences.

Mrs. Dasgupta had also enclosed a clipping from a fan magazine:

Guess who yours truly saw slipping off with bags and baggage (and that includes a female as well as suitcases) in the vicinity of the VIP lounge of DumDum Airport last week? You guessed it! None other than Mr. P. Bagchi, the super-villain whose performances are captivating and heady even when the films are buttressed with formulas and clichés. A reliable source tells us that petite, pretty and kittenish female accompanying him could be a superstar in her own right if she were to act, but that she believes "one star in the family is just enough to take. I'm content to be Mrs. P. Bagchi of Calcutta and Bombay for the present." Producers take note: her name is Pixie Ray and in our estimation there's still room for more Bengali beauties in the industry.

Mrs. Dasgupta had written over the clipping, in English to show her anger, DISGUSSTING.

Dimple read and reread the brief clipping, then she put it away in the old shoebox in which she stored all letters from her parents. Goddamnit, she said to herself, then repeated it aloud, startling herself with its passion. Now Pixie would probably live in a fancy apartment building on Park Street or Lord Sinha Road and do her hair in an elaborate knot like a Bengali actress and go to premiers in Bombay and meet all the famous people in government and business; she'd swing her diamond drop-earrings flirtatiously (Pixie had always known how to flirt, Dimple thought, though she'd never called it flirting back then) and drive off to a cocktail party where her actor husband would fix her a fresh lime and soda and tell excruciatingly funny jokes to very rich businessmen who would speak of their "associates" in Kuwait and the Gulf emirates. Pixie's life would be led like a film script: in life Prosanto Bagchi would not act as a villain.

Later in November, Ina Mullick began to bring her American friends over to the apartment on Bleecker Street. To Dimple they all looked alike; even their clothes were similar. She felt too shy to talk to them so she made coffee in a big pot and sat on the sofa and listened to them talk about sexism and day-care centers. They made their own cigarettes (Dimple worried that Amit would discover the stray tobacco strands between the sofa cushions and accuse her of entertaining men in the apartment; she was sure she could not explain the presence of women who could roll cigarettes with one hand while still gesturing with the other). Dimple had once taken Ina aside and asked if the hostess was supposed to provide the cigarettes as well as the coffee. In a Bengali movie about high society life, there had been waiters in white gloves circulating through the crowd with platters of cigarettes and fancy lighters. But Ina said that Americans liked to smoke their own brands.

Sometimes Milt Glasser came with Ina. He was growing a beard and it looked good on him; his face was so large, Dimple thought, that it needed a frame. It made him look older and more serious; it even brought out little wrinkles around his eyes. He looked more like an accountant or an architect. He also carried a bag, a heavy leather bag with shoulder straps and flaps. Dimple had expected a purse-carrying man to look effeminate, but Milt looked so manly that she thought of giving Amit a shoulder bag as a thirtieth birthday present. When Milt came she talked to him exclusively (he was less frightening than Ina's women friends), and played him her Suchitra Mitra tapes. But Milt did not come often enough.

On the morning that Dimple had received the letter about Pixie and her actor-husband, Ina Mullick came to the apartment with an American girl in a long suede skirt. The girl in suede was called Leni Anspach and she was slightly hunchbacked. She looked more hunchbacked when she was standing than when she was sitting on the sofa, almost lost among the large corduroy cushions, and she was standing at the moment and talking very quickly about her "poisoned relationship" with Ina. Dimple thought Leni's mouth was too large and squishy: it was like the baby calf liver under plastic wrap at the Grand Union. Dimple tried to make excuses for the mouth, told herself it was probably the strange lipstick color and the high-gloss finish, but the more she stared at Leni and took in the straight, thick eyebrows and the greasy, yellow hair, the more she wished Leni Anspach had not come.

Leni had jumped up from the sofa and was shaking her handcrafted earrings and stamping fiercely on the shaggy white rug and accusing Ina of undermining their beautiful relationship by flirting with Milt Glasser. Dimple would have liked to interrupt Leni, pull Ina to the bedroom and show her the clipping about Pixie and Prosanto Bagchi and say, in as calm a voice as she could muster, "Can you imagine? My best friend is about to become a superstar?" but Leni never paused, never gave Dimple a chance to break into her furious monologue.

Ina was denying the accusation vehemently and dropping cigarette ash all over the shaggy rug until Dimple was driven to cry in anguish, "Here, take an ashtray!" not because it was so hard to vacuum Marsha's rug but because Ina was so close to tears and it seemed so horrible of a hunchbacked girl with greasy hair to say such nasty things to a faithful Bengali wife like Ina. Dimple thrust the rhinoceros-shaped ashtray into Ina's hand so the fury would be deflected and Ina could regain her composure. But Leni Anspach was too quick for her, too vicious in the way she grabbed the ashtray and flung it on the rug and screamed that Dimple was a coward, that she had no right to worry about the rug and housework when she, Leni, was laying bare her soul to Ina. And Leni swung her neck from side to side in a hysterical pendulum motion, her nails clawed deep tracks on the suede skirt, and a ball of spit hung from the corner of her mouth. She screamed and screamed, and all the while Ina sat in a daze on the rug with the broken rhinocerous ashtray in her hand, mumbling, "Now see what you've done. We could have worked things out if you hadn't interfered." Dimple sat on the rug with her,

and all she could think was now it's too late to tell Ina
Mullick the marvelously shocking story about Pixie
marrying an actor. A fifty-three-year-old actor! So she
quietly plucked the ashtray from Ina's opened palm and
turned it over in her own hand several times to assess
the full damage. There was a large chip on the shoulder
and a larger one on the back and a hind leg had broken
off just below the joint. The horn, of course, was gone.
Somewhere in the deep pile of the rug, amidst all the
pins and needles that she'd never found but deeply
feared, were the chipped pieces of the china rhinoceros.
She decided it was best to regard the broken ashtray as
the end of an era in her own life. But with that decision
came a tightening of her throat and a sudden spasm of
crying that brought Ina to her side asking what in heav-
en's name was the matter. "Put water on, Leni," she
shouted to the American girl who still stood above them,
but Leni shouted back, "It's only a lousy *kitsch* ashtray,
for God's sake. I'll go down to Khanna's India Empo-
rium and buy her a dozen, okay?"

Dimple wished she had flung it on the rug herself,
or rather dropped it in a calculating way to show that
she understood what the other women were saying about
being exploited by housework and afraid of self-
expression and about avoiding confrontation. It would
have been such a relief to bury her face in the back of
Marsha's sofa and leave large dark brown damp stains
on the corduroy upholstery and to blame Milt Glasser
for dividing and conquering and causing this emotional
circus. But crying in front of the others, crying so hard
that the eyelids turned puffy and the cheeks looked
streaky like Leni's suede skirt, was more than she could
bear, so she said, "How silly I was. Such a little thing
really. Let me make some Darjeeling tea; I'm sure
that'll improve our tempers." She said it in her sweetest

voice. To say rude and nasty things to a total stranger required unnatural courage.

The kitchen was pitch-dark and warm. In the dark she took down the kettle, filled it and set it on the stove, then took out mugs and spoons and arranged them in a neat row on the counter. She hoped the water would take a long time to boil—she had filled the kettle to the brim—so she would not have to go back into the living room until Ina and Leni had finished screaming about confrontation and Milt Glasser. And as the darkness became gray instead of pitch-black and no longer disastrous, as familiar shapes of garbage can, breadbox, blender and Wheaties box emerged, as fear subsided and anger eased into the vacuum, she realized that she was ill. Illness did not disturb her when it could be apprehended through blameless physical symptoms as she now had: shortness of breath, nausea, sharp pains in back and stomach. Vomiting could be pleasurable; thinking of all the bathrooms she had vomited in she felt nostalgic, almost middle-aged. Leni and Ina did not understand her; they would never understand her. They stalked the future. She leaned over the kitchen sink, grasping the faucet expertly with her left hand and leaving the right free to maneuver an imaginary piston deep inside her throat. The piston moved, correct, efficient, not at all capricious, stopped for a few seconds as she took a deep breath, then moved again. But instead of the great gush Dimple had hoped for, only a thin trickle was expelled. It gravitated toward the drain, a small slimy pool full of bubbles. She was ashamed of it; it seemed more impersonal than a cooking stain. Still leaning over the sink, she ran cold water over her face so the women would not detect from its puffiness the intensity of her anger. Then she whispered, ''Why

Milt? She had no right to bring him into all this. He's a nice boy and he doesn't flirt.''

When the water came to a boil, Dimple steeped four instead of three teaspoons of tea leaves in the pregnant-bellied tea pot because it was a crisis situation and she knew crises called for a strong brew. A lacy trail of steam was visible around the lid of the teapot. She remembered having read somewhere—she had this despicable, compulsive habit of reading household hints in magazines, then ripping them out and throwing them into an old shoebox—that the tea leaves should be steeped in a lidless jar and then transferred to a conventional teapot. She could not remember or think or read anything but trivia. All her anger and her affection found their finest expression in cooking, though sometimes the recipes conspired against her sentiments.

The unfairness of what life had done to her overwhelmed Dimple. There would be no thrilling demolitions, merely substitutions. Her tactful domestic virtues and Amit's savings would accrue steadily and they would retire to Calcutta before they were sixty to lead circumspect lives, envied by those friends who had never left. And she was living the stories now that she would be telling for the next forty years! Sometimes, when reminiscence and security fought crepuscular battles in her mind, she would take her American appliances out of their careful wrappings and gaze at them in wonder as though they were relics of a prehistoric civilization.

The tea, still brewing in the awkward teapot, had turned black instead of the healthy brown Dimple had intended. She could guess its taste: bitter, cold and slightly abrasive under the tongue. Still it was her duty to carry the tea out into the living room and pretend serenity. The women offered to help her carry the tray, but she, convinced they were predators, kept them out of her kitchen. She began to think of her promise of tea as a promise of deliverance from indecent passions. With saintly obduracy, she plucked a tray from the highest shelf and crowded it with the apparatus of her exorcism, adding, like incense, two kinds of cookies and half a raisin and date cake to confuse the senses. Then she returned to the living room, where she heard Leni say, ''The moment I stopped wearing them in public I became a new woman.''

''Don't be daft,'' Ina said. ''You can't go around like that. You've got to be crazy.''

''Why?'' Leni cried. ''Why should I wear dentures for you or anybody? I feel so happy, so free, without them!'' She cupped her mouth with both hands and with a jerk, detached two rows of teeth, which she dropped with a clatter between the sugar bowl and the teapot on the tray. ''So there,'' she said, baring her gums.

''Dear God, I don't believe it,'' Ina whispered. Then, after two false starts, Leni and Ina fell into each other's arms. Like people in reconciliation scenes in television dramas, Dimple thought bitterly. It was not that she felt left out. Nor that she had never seen toothless women; they were common enough in India. Her own grandmother, a widowed vegetarian, had trained her gums to pulverize effortlessly beans, carrots and crackers. But on Leni Anspach, naked gums were unnatural, indecorous. The gums, horribly pink and shiny, like secret lips, only more lecherous and lethal, set themselves up as enemies of decent, parsimonious living. They challenged; they insulted. Dimple considered them unforgivable.

''I'm sure I make the best tea in Manhattan,'' she said. The women seemed not to hear her. They sat on the rug, sobbing and hugging, and discarding butts in the broken ashtray.

"And it's a special Calcutta blend," Dimple continued. Leni held her cup over her dentures, still not looking at Dimple, still smiling gummily at Ina. And Dimple poured. After Leni removed her cup Dimple kept on pouring, over the rim of Leni's cup, over the tray and the floating dentures till the pregnant-bellied tea pot was emptied and Leni and Ina were standing and shaking her, "Dimple, Dimple, stop it!"

She had not expected protest to be so enjoyable. She lay in bed, giggling at the memory of Leni's gaping mouth, Ina's squeals of delight turning to frenzy. Leni cried stupidly, "What did I say? What did I do?" even as Ina had taken Leni's hand and pulled her from the carpet and they had run out, hand in hand. Now, she savored the physical sensation, the curious sweetness at the root of her tongue, the chill, the goosebumps, as she waited for the enemy to regroup and attack.

Later, she thought of two more ways to die. One was to stand under a warm shower and slice open the jugular, though it would mean having to ask Amit where the jugular vein was, exactly, and he might get suspicious. He was a suspicious sort of person. The other was to squat near the kitchen cabinet where the cleaning fluids were, select an aerosol can of pesticide, open her mouth wide, air and spray for a very long time. She speculated if the pesticides came in different flavors as well as different scents—peppermint, wild cherry, lemon—like chewing gum. It was important for the body to look and smell good when discovered. The moment of discovery, the moment when someone came across her corpse and let out a shriek, obsessed her. It would not do to think of beetles and roaches on their shells, with frail legs jabbing the air. The exposed jugular vein was more aesthetic. She could see pretty jet sprays of pinkish blood. They flared toward the ceiling of the bathroom, then fell backward and ran down her breasts and shoulders. She would like to make one extravagant gesture in her life. If she only knew where the jugular was! What if Amit were to lie to her? It made nine ways to die altogether.

Two hours later, while Dimple was still creating moments of death, Ina Mullick came back carrying a shabby green tote bag. The bag was stuffed very full; she could barely grip the handles for the pile of clothes inside. They stood in the hall, with the tote bag between them, and listened to the radiator sputter. You had to know that the radiator sputtered in order to hear its soft sputter. Otherwise, it was just another sound in the apartment that had no apparent cause; in the beginning Dimple had wondered if it had been the plants. Finally Ina said, "I'm sorry. I just had to come back and tell you I was sorry."

Dimple stood with her head tilted slightly to one side and put her hand out on the radiator. Drāno, she thought; garbage bag; set fire to sari made of synthetic fiber; head in oven; nick wrist with broken glass in a sink full of scalding dishwater: starve; fall on bread knife while thinking of Japanese samurai revivals.

"No, it was my fault."

"I brought you a peace offering," Ina said. She was holding the tote bag out to Dimple.

"I think that girl didn't like my name," Dimple said as she took the bag from Ina. "She was laughing at me from the beginning."

"It's not your fault," Ina said. "We didn't choose our names. I'm sure I wouldn't be Ina Mullick if I had had anything to do with it."

"I am very attached to my name," Dimple said. "That girl had no right to laugh." She pulled out turtlenecks, bodysuits and three pairs of pants from the bag and hugged them against her bosom. "What's this?" she asked in a whisper. "You can't move in here." There was a stale odor of deodorant to the clothes.

"They're for you," Ina said. "I thought you might like to wear something out of this collection and walk down the block with me and have a pizza."

"I'm sorry," Dimple whispered. "There are some things I can't do. Wearing pants is one of them. I couldn't walk down the street in your pants and sweaters."

"Why are you whispering?" Ina demanded. "Why are you acting so guilty? Amit won't see you, if that's your main fear!"

"It's not that," Dimple said. "I just don't want to start all this. If I wear pants to eat pizza in the winter, who knows what I'll be wearing to eat at the Dairy Queen next summer."

"Okay, okay," Ina said. "Let's forget it. I was just trying to make you look normal and anonymous on Bleecker Street, that's all."

"But I feel more normal in a sari!" Dimple protested. "What's more normal and graceful than a sari?" She watched Ina stuff the clothes back into the shabby tote bag and squeeze the handles shut. She wore black leather gloves and a white vinyl coat with white fur trim. "You don't have to go away just because I won't wear your kind of clothes!" The trouble with Ina, Dimple thought, was that she had lost her patience. She just did not want to understand that Dimple would feel *naked* in Ina's clothes.

"I'd better go," Ina said. She was already halfway

out the front door. In her white coat and faded jeans
and scuffed shoes, she looked very pathetic, not at all
like Bijoy Mullick's wife. Her heels were worn down
sharply on the outer edges and gave her walk a strange
bobbing motion, like a goat's. "Dimple," she said,
"I'm very sorry if Leni laughed at your name. But don't
think I laugh at you. The truth is, I envy you a little."
She hefted the bag, and halfway toward the elevator
turned to call, "I'll phone you tomorrow."

"Why?" Dimple asked. But the elevator door closed
on Ina's answer.

At 4:38 by the travel-clock in the bedroom she admitted to herself that she was scared. Everything scared
her: the sputtering of the radiators, the brown corduroy
sofa with depressions where Leni and Ina had sat before
they slipped into more relaxed positions on the floor,
the needles in the rug, the ironing board in the hall
waiting to fall if you walked too close, the Leger prints,
the blender under its terry towel cover, the cactus that
had not flowered the way it was supposed to, the
smudgy wide windows behind the dining table. She was
sure something terrible was about to happen though she
had not had any experience predicting disasters.

Premonitions should be accompanied by courage and
caution; they are cruel in a person whose instincts have
been worn down by overuse. Dimple felt helpless and
old. She wished Ina had stayed though she was always
miserable when Ina stayed. Ina would have known how
to cope with disaster. And with the fear of disaster. But
Ina could not have consoled her. That was the hateful
thing about Ina: she promised happiness, independence, love, but no consolation. Then she panicked: her
need to be consoled was so immense, so violent that it
could only crush her. She tried to deflect its course.

She read the backs of cereal boxes that promised FREE INSIDE! She ate two forkfuls of leftover curried cauliflower before throwing up. But the panic was still there. Also the hate. Life should have treated her better, should have added and subtracted in different proportions so that she was not left with a chimera. Amit was no more than that. He did not feed her reveries; he was unreal. She was furious, desperate; she felt sick. It was as if some force was impelling her towards disaster; some monster had overtaken her body, a creature with serpentine curls and heaving bosom that would erupt indiscreetly through one of Dimple's orifices, leaving her, Dimple Basu, splattered like a bug on the living-room wall and rug. The cataclysm embarrassed her.

In times of crisis, one must act cool. She had heard someone say that, someone whose voice was like ice cubes colliding against glass. It might have been on television: it was getting harder and harder to distinguish between what she had seen on TV and what she had imagined. She thought of the television set as her only friend; it was so undemanding, it gave and gave and asked nothing of her in return. It could have been Amit who had talked of staying cool in crises or it could have been Nixon or even Milt Glasser's special hero, Walt Frazier. A half-remembered line kept coming back to her: I rest kool, I krisis kool and she saw Amit in a Macy's suit sitting next to Johnny Carson. Amit was good in emergencies; he could arrange last-minute railway tickets for friends, produce candles and flashlights during unexpected power cuts, joke with strikers in Dalhousie Square and stop them from burning the company car. If she could think of Amit for a whole minute, just shut her eyes and think of nothing else but Amit, try to picture his hair, his eyes, the tiny mole on the left side of his neck just above the collar, if she could

fine-tune the picture, she might learn from him how to
manage crises without losing her charm or temper. Ina
said that skipping rope and taking vitamin B-12 were
good for the nerves. Dimple had not mentioned that the
last time she'd skipped rope she'd lost a fetus and two
pints of blood. And vitamin overdoses, she'd read, could
be poisonous. Better to imitate the managerial cool of
Bijoy Mullick, the engineering cool of Jyoti Sen and
Amit. When she forced herself to visualize his face,
then slowly his body, even his feet (by the time she'd
gotten to the feet the head was just a balloon), Amit
became an *Esquire* ad: a young man in front of a type-
writer smiling confidently at her saying, "and while
you're up, get me a . . ." It was outrageous that she
could not separate him from the men on Johnny Carson's show or the young men showing off liquor and
clothes in shiny magazines. Desperately she attacked
the magazines on the coffee table because they were his
magazines and would help her to separate the man from
the ads and TV commercials. But he kept leering at her
in cowboy hat and Levis, smoking menthol-flavored
cigarettes, or sun-tanned and bare-bodied, running into
Caribbean waters. Once she thought she almost had him
in a Dewar's Profile:

Amit Kumar Basu
Home: New York City (or should she cancel that and
put Calcutta?)
Age: Twenty-nine
Profession: Mechanical Engineer
Hobbies: Cricket, also rearing parrots
Last Accomplishment: Decision to emigrate
Quote: Husbands should not permit their wives to wear
pants. A healthy society and mutual respect are based

on the clear distinction between the appearance and the functions of the sexes.

But she could not find him anywhere in the apartment, not in the bedroom closet where his new $140 American suit and sports coat hung with his two Barkat Ali summer suits, not even in the bathroom where the mirror was still flecked with his shaving cream or toothpaste and the last glob of sandalwood soap that she had brought from Calcutta was melting in a blue plastic soap dish. She could not find him anywhere and it was only six o'clock. She thought of six o'clock as the hour when good wives like Meena Sen in Queens were wiping counter tops clean, then checking on the baby to make sure it was sleeping on its stomach and finally tiptoeing out of the room with an armful of damp diapers to iron. For God's sake, she remembered that Ina had once asked, what kind of woman irons diapers! So she called Ina before the impulse (or courage; she was not sure which was the better word) dissipated and asked without preliminaries "Were you really serious about lending me your clothes? Or was it some kind of a joke?" and she heard Ina say in a slow, unmodulated voice, "Why don't you come on over? Milt's here, and a friend of his who's just come back from a year in Bhuvaneswar," and Dimple thought that Ina and she were always asking questions of each other because neither one had any answers. She heard herself make excuses for not coming over to meet the boy—he was called Larry Friedkin—from Bhuvaneswar; then she wrapped her sari tightly around her breasts and shoulders and stood with an eye screwed to the peephole of the front door, waiting for Amit to fit his key in the lock.

* * *

The footsteps were too firm. And imprudent. Amit's were gentler and more cautious. She felt disaster-prone: a woman whose husband was always late from work.

Dimple let him ring twice, then opened the door a crack. The man who had winked at Ina in the elevator slipped in, like a cat, and smiled at her. He held a bicycle decal in one hand (reminding her of FREE INSIDE! cereal box temptations) and a bottle of wine in the other.

"I thought you might like this," he said, offering her the decal. "It's some Hindu god, isn't it?"

She thought it would have been worse if he had been a stranger. Without touching the decal, she examined it. "It's Krishna," she said firmly. "You see the flute? Yes, it's definitely Krishna." The scene was almost familiar. She played it many times before: Milt Glasser arriving unexpectedly and staying for dinner. Or a rapist with gaudy tie and black mustache. The rapists never got beyond the dark hall. The rooms, especially the kitchen and bathroom, were inviolable.

"Remember me?" the man asked. He put his wine down on the telephone table in the hall. In the cone of light from Marsha's lamp (a clever thing made from an S-trap and a cheese board) she noticed that his sideburns were uneven.

After that there were many more questions. Dimple's English deteriorated before the volley of his words, reducing her to smiles, nods and grunts. Silence seemed to disconcert him; he filled the pauses between questions with nervous laughs. His presence in the apartment mystified Dimple; if she had not seen him earlier, carrying groceries in the elevator, she would have assumed he was a creature of nightmare. But any man who carried celery had to be real, and if she were to dial Ina's number, she was sure Ina would authenticate the man's reality. To chase away the last lingering doubts, she studied him covertly—his face was unnaturally brown, his hair a reddish yellow—but the mystery remained. He did not ask to come into the living room, but he did not go away either.

His curiosity frightened her. He asked seven questions on the weather alone, four on the monsoons and three on Calcutta winter temperatures, converting Centigrade into Fahrenheit in his head and asking her to confirm his answers. The questions exhausted Dimple. She knew nothing of latitudes and wind directions, and felt bad that she could not satisfy his need for precision. Her vagueness astonished him. Sometimes, Dimple thought, he suspected her of deviousness, of feigning ignorance to tease him. Then he sounded peeved, disapproving. She could not endure disapproval, not even a stranger's. So when the man slipped in a question about Ina between two on comparative rainfall figures, she seized it eagerly. She heard herself say, in halting English and with an unfamiliar titter, "No, no, you have it all wrong; she isn't my roommate. You see, I'm *Mrs*. Dimple Basu. Mrs. Mullick doesn't live here."

The man looked very discouraged, apologetic, even a little sick, though he continued to ask two or three more questions about Ina. But the questions seemed improvised rather than ruthlessly persistent. He had trouble with phrases; he mispronounced words. Dimple thought that the man did not really want to know any more about Ina, that for him Ina was probably an ephemeral, unsatisfying topic compared to Indian monsoon patterns, and having exhausted the weather he was anxious to leave. So she created longer and longer pauses in the conversation, giving him decent openings for casual farewell rituals. She considered herself a master of situations in which passions are discreetly restrained. Ina, Dimple knew, would either have led the man to the deep, brown sofa or shoved him out into the hall when he showed her the decal. That was the trouble with people like Leni and Ina who believed in frankness, happiness and freedom; they lacked tolerance, and they abhorred discussions about the weather.

In the next apartment there was the sound of doors being opened and closed, then faint screams. Dimple shuddered. The man picked up his bottle of wine, saying, "It's late; I have to rush." At the front door, he had some problem with the lock, and Dimple had to let him out.

Dimple stayed in the hall, rearranging telephone directories, until the man's footsteps were inaudible. Amit would be home soon and she would have to decide if she should tell him about the intruder. It was all in the telling, because nothing had happened. It had been a neighborly act, and Amit prized all contact, however marginal, with American neighbors. But her imagination, inflamed by too many hours in front of the TV, pictured what might have been. And alone in the dark apartment, Dimple collapsed in terror.

The next morning Dimple received a letter from her mother and a phone call from Meena Sen. Her mother said that the boy with water in his head had died; he had been run over by a bus. Dimple wondered if the water had come spurting out in yellowish sprays and had hit the passengers holding on near the windows. That was all she could visualize as she read and reread the paragraph of the boy's being run over. She was ashamed of herself because she wanted to cry, wanted to shut herself up in the bathroom and try cutting her jugular with a razor blade under the warm shower, but all she worried about was how the passengers on the bus had felt as the head was broken or crushed.

When Meena called and asked Amit and Dimple to come over for dinner that evening and meet two new Bengali couples who had just arrived from Calcutta, she was still thinking of the water-soaked brain that must have been spewed out under the tires of the bus. She said that she and Amit would love to come and would eight-thirty be too late? But she was thinking that probably a lot of people on the bus got sick after seeing it happen and were late for work.

Between six-thirty and eight, she showered, dressed in a new printed silk sari, urged Amit to have more tea and cookies and stared out of the living-room window at Puerto Rican girls on Bleecker Street below. They looked devastatingly like Indians. If she had succumbed to Ina's temptation, she would have looked like one of those Puerto Rican girls on the street corner and people walking by would not have known the difference, would not have known that she was a sensitive young woman from Ballygunje and that her best friend had married a famous movie star and made it into *Stardust*.

All the way on the subway to Queens she stared discreetly at black and brown girls in leather jackets, allocating her gaze to posters or the dark tunnels when the girls stared back at her. Sometimes she put herself in their places, pretending that Amit with his oily hair and thin little mustache was a "dude" with a comb in his hip pocket, and making up stories that she would not have made up if she had thought of herself as Dimple Basu or even Dimple Dasgupta. When they arrived at the Sens' apartment, Dimple was still seeing herself as a high-breasted black woman in thick gold earrings and very short curly hair.

"We were just talking about you," Meena Sen laughed as she opened the door. "We were just saying how much nicer it would have been if you had found an apartment here.'' There was a smell of frying onions and garlic in the hall, and the high-pitched laughter of Bengalis having fun. She took Dimple by the arm and led her into the living room and introduced her to the new couples who said they had heard so much about her from Meena. The room looked much smaller than she had remembered and the sofa that she and Amit used to sleep on had been covered with an old silk sari embroidered all over with little green peacocks. There was also a new set of plastic flowers—blue roses—in a short blue and white vase.

Jyoti shouted from his corner, ''What have you been doing to your wife, Amit old chap? She's looking so thin! Is he trying to starve you, or what? Look how nice and fat Meena is, even after the baby!'' Then there was the sound of a toilet flushing and Mrs. Bhattacharya bounced in, wearing a pink nylon georgette sari and ankle socks, and cried, ''How nice to see you, strangers. But why are you looking so pale and sick? Are you helping to explode the population like Mrs. Sen?''

Dimple sat between two of the new people and stared covertly at the other two new ones. Mr. and Mrs. Roy were short, plump and dark and looked more like brother and sister than husband and wife. Dimple had a theory that after a while married couples began to resemble each other. It was inevitable that in a few months or a few years—she did not know exactly when the symbiotic process started or if it varied from couple to couple (with her own parents, the earliest married photos showed a tall, lean young man with a mustache, and his short, gaunt wife; now both seemed short and fat, wore the same kind of glasses, and her father had shaved off the mustache when she was ten years old)—she would acquire Amit's way of moving and speaking.

She would become his faithful imitator. Mr. Roy was younger than Amit; Mrs. Roy a little older than Dimple.

Mrs. Roy said, "I always thought people got fairer in a cold climate, but I seem to be getting darker. I mean I've never been so dark!" She had a whining voice. She held her hand up in the light, but everyone politely looked away.

Mrs. Bhattacharya said, "That is a false theory. When you've been here as long as my husband and I— it will be seventeen years in May—you see that the climate makes no difference at all. In fact, you will go out in the sun here when you would never go out in Calcutta."

"I see," said Mrs. Roy.

"If that theory were true," Mrs. Bhattacharya continued, "then Mr. Bhattacharya would be as white as marble. He just got back from two weeks in Alaska. He works for Exxon."

"I see," said Mr. Roy.

Jyoti said that the Roys were staying with them, sleeping on the same sofa-bed the Basus had slept on. She could not imagine Mrs. Roy lying awake at night or breaking the plastic flowers. She could not imagine Jyoti Sen talking to her of passion at four o'clock in the morning.

Dimple would have liked to talk to Mrs. Guha who was sitting, very aloof and elegant, on a kitchen chair in the living room and nervously rubbing her fingernails together. But she was too shy to move from the sofa and take a new position on the floor. So she sat between the Roys and tried not to be jealous that Jyoti was bending over Mrs. Guha's head and offering her orange juice and *kabob* balls that she said she did not want. The woman was very pretty and very smartly dressed, with long kiss curls on her cheeks and a blouse that had sequins all over. Dimple felt underdressed and unfashionable in spite of her new sari; her clothes had been fashionable the summer before but now she felt she had lost touch with Calcutta. In a year or two she would probably wear ankle socks and synthetic saris like Mrs. Bhattacharya's.

Mrs. Roy said, "If I had known it would be so cold I'd have refused to come! He tricked me into believing New York had pleasant weather. Do you know the trouble I have keeping my stockings up?"

Mrs. Bhattacharya said, "I recommend ski slacks under the sari when the weather gets really rough. Some girls try to be modern and wear pantyhose, but I personally find that quite unforgivable."

And Jyoti said something naughty about pantyhose and everyone laughed. Before Jyoti could finish another joke about women with fat legs in stockings, the women disappeared into the bedroom to look at the new baby and Archana. But Jyoti followed them in and interrupted their conversation about how difficult it was to bring up nice Bengali girls in America with the constant exposure to bad influences, saying "Now, now, we don't want any separation of the sexes here. We believe in being modern!" Then he sat next to Mrs. Guha on the bed piled high with coats and discoursed on the properly liberated state of women in early Vedic India.

At dinner Dimple managed to sit on the sofa beside Jyoti and she would have been happy, she thought, if only Mrs. Guha had not sat on the other side of Jyoti on the same sofa and looked so irresistible in her long, wispy kiss curls. Poor Mr. Guha was still gleaning job information from Amit; he was a small, wiry-haired fellow who looked more like an office boy than a graduate engineer. Amit was wearing his new American suit and looked very well established. He sat on a cushion on the floor and his knees jutted out at uneven angles. Dimple was afraid that the plate he was balancing on his knees would slope down into his lap and ruin his pants. He was putting on weight and the pockets of his pants flared out on either side, revealing white linings and tight crease marks. When he sat, there was an unpleasant fold of fat straining at his shirt buttons. She wondered what it was about the Mookerjis' apartment in Manhattan that made Amit fatter and her thinner instead of leveling out their differences and making them look like happy brother and sister. She watched Amit intently so that she could remember how he ate, how his fingers—he had hairs on two joints of each finger—curled around the fried rice and made firm little balls, how his chin worked up and down quickly and his mouth made little noises, how he spat out the lemon peel and chicken bones. She wanted to remember him exactly as he was—not as a face on TV or in an ad but as a very solid person sitting on the Sens' second-hand rug chewing and spitting with vigor while telling Messers Roy and Guha about the tight job market for industrial engineers.

"Stop arguing!" ordered Meena Sen with a laugh. "Try my *kala jamuns*; I made them from a new recipe. You're only talking and eating nothing. I'll think I'm a bad hostess if all the *kala jamuns* don't disappear." She went on to tell the other wives about a new Bengali cookbook she had just bought; it was written especially for Bengalis abroad and gave very clever instructions on what to substitute for unobtainable ingredients.

On the way home, on a deserted part of the subway platform, Amit leaned against a defunct candy dispenser and threw up the *kala jamuns*. She was terribly embarrassed. "I wish you would buy a car," she said. "I'm sure a second-hand car doesn't cost that much and we could rent parking space from somebody."

"I'm dying and you talk to me about buying cars!" Amit clutched his stomach with gloved fingers and looked very angry.

Dimple was afraid a policeman would come and create a scene about vomiting in public. She was afraid of New York policemen; they reminded her of sirens on the street, drunks in doorways, belligerent junkies. She held Amit's hand and walked him to a more crowded part of the platform so people would not connect the mess on the ground with him. Amit said that she would find his life insurance policy in the drawer of the night table and that he wanted to be cremated and have his ashes scattered over the Ganges. She wondered what sort of container one kept such ashes in on a transatlantic trip; plastic bags or the kind of plastic box with tight-fitting lids that she kept leftovers in? And what happened to the bits of bone and organs that were charred but not totally consumed? The train came just as she decided they were premature and indiscreet questions to ask Amit.

By early December Dimple knew that the world was divided into Friends and Enemies and that the Enemies outnumbered the Friends by a hundred to one and the odds were becoming increasingly long. One morning when she had been standing at the front door with her eye sort of fitted into the peephole of the door—that way she could ward off the man who fumbled with keys near her front door—she saw Ina Mullick and Milt Glasser leaning on her doorbell with the tip of an umbrella.

Ina came in, dumped her shabby tote bag on the head

of a wooden doll from Saurashtra that Marsha had said she was very fond of and said to Dimple, "Do you remember Leni? Well, she left yesterday for Katmandu and points unknown. I don't know how they do it, how they just pack up and leave, do you?"

Milt bent over Dimple and put his huge hands on her shoulders and brought his face very close (she noticed that he had acne scars on his nose) and she stood very still, leaning slightly against the wall, not sure if he was about to kiss her and what she should do if he did kiss her on the cheek or mouth. But he seemed content to draw close, then stand in front of her with his hands on her shoulders.

Ina said, "I don't think you like us anymore. I think you are just pretending to like us because you hate to be rude. I wish you would be outrageously rude just once in your life. Go on, try to throw us out. For God's sake, try to be spontaneous, will you?"

Dimple wriggled out of Milt Glasser's hold and walked to a safe corner near the window, between the cactus and the ivy, and said, quite hotly, "Of course, I like you. Who said I don't like you?"

Ina said, "You don't have to get so terribly defensive with me. I'm your friend, remember? I know why you let me come so often. Because you can't say no. You think that's rude, and you'd rather die than be rude."

Dimple leaned forward and tested the soil in the pots with her finger, but since she had no idea what kind of plants required what kind of dryness, she knew she was playing for time to think up a retort. So far five plants had developed brown spots and two had mold around the roots though she dared not throw them out. She said, "If you *are* my friend, then how come you are trying to hurt me like this? How come you're telling me to be rude?"

Milt Glasser came over to her corner and touched her elbow and said, "Easy now, take it easy," and made a sign to Ina, then moved his hand from her elbow all the way down to her wrist. "Don't pay any attention to her." Then louder, turning to Ina, "Lay off, Ina. I mean it."

She let the hand rest on her wrist because it was such a nice hand, the kind of hand that could never do anything rude. She said, "I can't keep up with you people. I haven't read the same kinds of books or anything. You know what I mean, Ina, don't you? I just like to cook and watch TV and embroider, and would you believe it, I got ninety-eight percent once in my needlework class?"

"Bravo!" cried Ina Mullick from the sofa where she was sitting cross-legged. "And what else does our little housewife do?"

"You're making fun of me," Dimple screamed. "Who do you think you are? What gives you the right to walk into my house and make fun of me like that?"

"Are you telling me to get out?" Ina asked. She pouted and uncrossed her legs. "Well, if that's the way you treat friends in this house . . ." Ina walked to the closet in the hall, wriggled into her white vinyl coat, zipped up her knee-high boots and said from the front door, "Milt Glasser, you'll come with me right now if you know what's good for all three of us."

Milt stayed by the cactus and moved his big hand from Dimple's wrist to her palm. She noticed that he had no hair on his fingers, but the veins stood out on the back of his hand like maps of the Ganges.

"Go, Ina," he said. "When you get your head screwed on right, come back."

When Ina had left, shutting the door very angrily

behind her, Milt said that he liked to cook also and that his mother had gone to school with Julia Child.

"You mean *the* Julia Child on television?" Dimple asked incredulously. "Do you really know her?" She had thought the people on TV existed in the tubes and transistors; she could not think of them as riding subways, being hungry, looking for adapter-converters at Macy's, going to school with Milt's mother.

"Of course," Milt answered airily. He pulled her with him to the kitchen and said he would show her how to make a Julia Child special chocolate mousse and began to talk in the panting, breathless voice of the gourmet superstar. He broke four eggs, joking as he worked, and separated the whites and yolks in Marsha's glass bowls, taking care to scoop out flecks of yellow from the bowl of whites along with broken bits of shell. "The tricky part, sweetheart, is to beat the yolks while you dribble the hot syrup in this gook here." And because she seemed to stiffen at the word *sweetheart*, he said with a soft laugh, "I was doing a weak Humphrey Bogart–via–Woody Allen imitation. Okay, sweetheart?"

Dimple giggled after that, giggled as if she were a one-woman audience at a comic movie, and Milt continued in his Bogart voice, alternating with his Howard Cosell, his street dude, his Woody-Allen-impressing-a-lady-with-a-chocolate mousse for which he ended up dabbing her cheeks with egg yolks and she thought of Archana fingerpainting in nursery school and dabbed Milt right back with melted chocolate and butter.

Half an hour later, they sat side by side on the brown sofa with their faces grubby and listened to Kanika Banerjee and Hemanta Kumar records; an hour later she fed him warm spoonfuls of mousse and told him how she slept all day because she was afraid to go out alone but that she did not really fall asleep because who could sleep for nineteen out of twenty-four hours and that she loved having friends drop in so that she would not stare up at the ceiling and wait for it to come down and crush her.

At six, Milt said, "Ciao, honey. I've got a date with Walt Frazier," picked up his parka and left. At seven Amit came home and showered before saying a word to her. When he had showered and put on his clean, handloomed *kurta pajama*, she sat on the sofa beside him and flirtatiously fed him a bowl of chilled chocolate mousse. "Honey, do you like my Julia Child special?"

"I hope you don't mind us dropping in without calling," Meena said to Dimple at about four o'clock the next afternoon.

"Of course not. You know I'm not a formal sort of person."

"Mrs. Roy had to come down to buy boots so we thought we'd come over and at least say hello."

"We can't stay very long, Mrs. Basu," said Mrs. Roy. She sat on the sofa but refused to take off her cloth coat with its narrow fake fur collar, though she unbuttoned the two top buttons.

"I was afraid you might be doing something," apologized Meena Sen. "We thought of calling from the store to warn you. You know how particular people here are about calling before dropping in."

"Everyone's so formal here," sighed Mrs. Roy. She had slender stockinged feet, which she rubbed against the ridged texture of the corduroy upholstery. "Back home if you feel like visiting someone you just go. But here . . ."

"You must stay for a cup of tea, Mrs. Roy," Dimple said.

"Oh, no," Mrs. Roy said. "We must get back before the rush hour. We're carrying too many packages."

"I insist," Dimple said, smiling. "The water's almost ready. It won't take a minute."

"I've left Archana and the baby with Mrs. Guha," Meena Sen said. "I want to get back before they start giving her too much trouble."

"I would feel guilty leaving my child with someone," said Mrs. Roy, "but what can you do carrying a baby and holding on to another one and *then* carrying all the packages? Really, it's impossible to do anything here. How nice it would be to pile everything into a rickshaw and tell the fellow *chalo*, *jaldi-jaldi*. Things just aren't convenient over here." She had begun to rub her feet with her hands to keep them warm. "I do hate to wear shoes and boots. My feet feel so imprisoned."

Dimple disappeared into the kitchen to make tea and scoop out leftover chocolate mousse into pretty glass bowls.

"The doorbell just rang," Mrs. Roy shouted from the sofa.

"Did it really?"

"Yes, I heard it too," said Meena Sen. "The doorbell just rang."

"Oh, it's probably some kids," Dimple said from the kitchen. When the doorbell rang again, she said, "It happens every afternoon. That and wrong numbers on the telephone." She brought the tea things on a tray and set up little tables for the two women. There was a third ring, which they all decided to ignore.

"What's with the Mullicks?" Meena asked with her mouth full of mousse. "I haven't seen them for such a long time. They used to come over quite often, you know; come over without calling or anything. We used to be very friendly."

"I don't know."

"You're sure we haven't put you out too much? We haven't kept you from doing something important?"

"I never do anything important," said Dimple.

"It seemed like such a good idea since we were in Manhattan."

"If you're in Queens, just come on over. Meena-di will tell you how to get to our place. And Mrs. Guha is in the same building. It's really like a little Bally-gunje."

"I'd love to," Dimple said. She wrote down Mrs. Roy's address and phone number in a mushroom-shaped address book on the phone table. While she was standing there, the phone rang. Sinister laughter on the other end, Milt's "Shadow" voice, she hoped. She hung up.

"Don't bother to call beforehand, Mrs. Basu. We don't stand on formality."

"You must drop in on me, too," said Meena Sen. "You owe me a visit now."

"I'd like to very much," said Dimple. "I'll try next week."

Dimple pushed the shopping cart between the aisles and wondered what she was doing in borrowed clothes on a Tuesday morning in mid-December with Milt Glasser in the Grand Union. The clothes belonged to Marsha. She had taken them out of the bedroom closet—a printed sweater and blue jeans that were too long for her—because Milt had told her to. On top of all that finery she had worn Prodosh's windbreaker. She had no idea that dressing up in other people's clothes could be so much fun. She felt like an enemy agent in disguise in her borrowed get-up. A little ahead of her, with his hands on cans of mandarin oranges and pine-apple rings, Milt Glasser was full of ways to live on city, state or federal projects. Milt Glasser knew how to apply for things, knew about consulting, advising, accessing; he seemed to have a dozen careers and at least as many specializations, but he admitted he also had none at all. All he admitted was that he had friends, contacts, "marks" in city government, in the media, in the universities, in publishing, and that if large amounts of money were coming into New York in any of a dozen different fields, he had a good chance of getting part of it. He was, to her, America.

"You're not helping me," Dimple complained. "Should I take the pitted cherries or should I take the apricots?"

"Use some of that fabled oriental will power," he advised, and lobbed two small cans into her cart.

"It's not fair," Dimple complained. "Amit always tells me what to buy. We always discuss before he makes the selection. You're letting me do all the hard work." She wheeled her cart at a reckless speed to the frozen food section and fended off a fat woman who was about to reach for a frozen cheesecake on the shelf above Dimple's head. "Lemon or strawberry?" she yelled at Milt Glasser who was lagging behind. "I love them both so I don't care which one we get." When Milt did not yell back his choice, she put two pies in the shopping cart and wheeled ferociously out to the crowded area where he was examining hamburger and beef liver. She thought even the cart and its contents were part of her disguise: there were no cabbages, no cauliflowers and shiny eggplants, no see-through bags of orange lentils. This was an American cart; there were two large packs of pinkish red hamburgers—she realized she had never really looked at hamburger before—two large plastic-wrapped mounds, ridged and marbled and dripping blood. Even the celery leaves beneath were brownish with blood.

"Hey, I forgot," Milt said suddenly. "Are you vegetarian?"

"No, I eat fish and chicken," Dimple said. But she thought it would be fun to take the hamburger meat home, knead it like dough, make funny shapes with it, throw it up like a ball, then catch it before it splattered on the floor. In her borrowed clothes she felt she could risk anything and get away with it. "Also mutton," she said.

When they got home, she helped Milt make hamburgers—the pinkish meat got under her nails and for a while she feared Amit would be able to smell it on her for days to come—and she ate almost a whole one with mustard and relish, and waited until Milt had left before rushing to the bathroom and throwing it up. With her forehead on the edge of the toilet bowl between heaves, she thought it was a small price to pay for all the things she had done since moving into Manhattan.

That night Amit looked up from his crossword puzzle and said, "You used to be a lot of fun; you used to pester me to take you out and get a pizza or a gaucho pie; you know, *do* things. But now you just want to stay at home and you don't even watch television. What's wrong, for God's sake?"

Dimple said that there was nothing wrong. But Amit would not believe her. He said, "I know there's something wrong. What do you take me for, a goddamn fool or something? I can tell something's happened to you; you've changed in the last few months. You even look different."

She walked over to the television and turned it on and then went back to the sofa and held her head between her palms and asked, "Is that better? Do I look more usual now?"

And Amit said, "You're trying to pick a quarrel. Goddamnit, I try to be nice; I try to act concerned after a hard day's work and what happens—you want to nag and quarrel. I don't have to put up with all this, you know."

A woman in an evening dress on a talk show said, "I always go for the groin. I find that a fail-safe method."

Dimple went to bed. She did not want to watch television; it was becoming the voice of madness. The bedroom was full of street light; she placed Amit's pillow over her eyes and chanted her nine ways to die. A tenth way eluded her.

In January, the day after the first heavy snowfall, she sat on a bench in the playground in front of the apartment building because both the cactus and the ivy in the brass pot had developed incurable brown spots and would have to be thrown away. For a while there were four big boys in the fenced-in area, and they did not look cold. She was very cold though she was wearing a long-sleeved silk shirt and a fisherman's sweater and Amit's nylon socks under a pair of Marsha's shoes. She wore a pair of Amit's Barkat Ali pants, which seemed tissue-thin. The boys were digging in a corner where the sandbox had been all fall. Dimple thought that they did not look as if they belonged in the playground; they looked too old and their fathers were probably not professors and when they had finished digging they would hit her on the head with their shovels. It would be a novel way to die—she'd run out of devising ways on her own, trusting only to the random energy of the city— more immediately painful than freezing to death but more efficient. She walked up to the boys and watched them dig for a long time, but when it seemed quite clear to her that they did not want to have anything to do with her, she went back to the bench and warmed her toes by rubbing the shoes against the snow.

At six-thirty when Amit found her, she said, "If I had had *lined* gloves, it wouldn't have been so bad. Why didn't you buy me lined gloves? You want me to die. I know; you're just waiting for me to die."

He backed away from her and nearly tripped over a toy spade. Bewildered, she pursued him. Could he not see through her simulated venom? Did he not realize that she had set a test for him by sitting in the darkest corner of the playground? "Why do you hate me?" she cried.

"Why?" Amit asked. In the dark she could not tell if he was angry or about to cry. "Why in public, goddamnit?"

"There's nothing wrong with sitting on a public bench and waiting for one's husband, is there?" Dimple countered. She seemed to be waiting for events that failed to occur or occurred unnoticed. Her life was slow, full of miscalculations.

"I don't want to discuss it," Amit said, pulling her toward the elevator. Then as he neared the lighted rectangle of the entrance and the superintendent nodded in his direction, he added, "We'll talk about it upstairs, if you like."

"Why are you so upset? What's the matter with you?" she asked loudly, letting him drag her because her feet were numb in the borrowed shoes.

"I'm not upset," Amit retorted. When the elevator doors shut on the superintendent's dour face, he said in a belligerent voice, "It's you who's upset. Let's not get *that* confused, okay?"

She let him get away with that because she was so tired and it was too hard to talk about despair and death in an elevator. She felt dizzy, and chillier now then she had when she had sat in the playground. Amit stood beside her, his finger still on the button to prevent disobedience from the elevator.

How odd, how marvelous, Dimple thought, if the man who had winked at Ina should suddenly stop the elevator and enter it and wink unequivocally at her. She rode the last two floors expectantly. When the man did not appear, it was obvious to her that there would be no accidental rescue from Amit's wrath. He looked fidgety, harassed, wronged. One arm around her shoulder in poor imitation of affection, he was pushing her down the hall. So she escaped from his hold, shouting, "Leave me alone!" at the doors of other apartments, at the incinerator chute, at the Saurashtra doll in the hall and the bicycle decal by the telephone; she shouted it in the bathroom while he turned on the shower, then whispered it while the steam haloed her naked body. It was the first time she had stood naked in the tub in front of her husband. Shame, she discovered, was a sobering emotion.

She had expected Amit to be unreasonable, to argue and scold, but he said nothing, even smiled in a poor imitation of understanding. He helped her from the shower, dried her, found clean sheets and remade the bed. And when she lay stiffly on the sheets, he spread her hair like streamers on either side of the pillow.

"Why in a public place?" he demanded softly. "My position isn't that secure here, you know. Any kind of funny business gets put into your file and when it comes time to renew the alien residency, they might just cancel it. Next time, let's discuss it at home before you do something mad. At least wait till I get home, okay?"

Then she heard the bedsprings creak softly, the door open and shut again, the noise of water running in the sink and the faint rattle of tea things being loaded on a tray by a clumsy person.

After he had left the room she gave herself what she thought was probably half an hour, then switched on the table lamp, took a piece of paper and a ball-point pen out of a drawer in the night table and listed the reasons why she was unhappy.

1. The plants were dying
2.
3.
4.
5.

It was no use; it was too hard to be honest in writing. If you wrote something down, it was proof that you had really thought of it or felt it. You were trapped. She would not let that happen; she would not let them catch her out. She would *say* the reasons to herself because there was no way of proving that she had actually said it. It would be just her word against someone else's. All the reasons why she was unhappy. Except that now that she was actually ready to think about it, she wasn't so sure that she was unhappy after all. For instance, she didn't want to be like Ina Mullick (Ina said that she had gone to a C-R group on 116th Street and taken off her clothes and shown them her hernia scar so people wouldn't call her beautiful all the time), and she didn't want to be like Meena Sen or Mrs. Roy and live in a little Ballygunje ghetto. Then why was she so unhappy?

Two days later, as Dimple was sitting in front of a mirror in the bedroom and putting on her gold choker to go to a Saraswati *pujah* celebration uptown, Amit

asked, "Why didn't you tell me you were unhappy?"
Instead of trying to work things out for herself on the
cold park bench and almost freezing to death, he said,
she should have unburdened her worries to him and he
would have explained that it was culture shock and that
culture shock happened all the time to Indian wives; it
wasn't a serious thing and it certainly wasn't one of
those famous "breakdowns" that American wives were
fond of having. He promised her a trip to Calcutta by
charter flight, though he hated to part with five hundred
dollars. "If we see Khanna tonight, I'll ask him about
cheap fares. We could go for three weeks or so. If you
like, you could stay on for two or three months. I'd
come back to work."

"I was too tired to tell you," Dimple answered, then
asked Amit to help her fasten the choker so it would
not suddenly slip off. The choker was her favorite piece
of jewelry, part of the wedding dowry. It was heavy,
hung with gold squares and gold discs and sharp gold
fronds. She saved it for special occasions; it made her
feel very grand and married because she was certain
only married women could afford chokers. "Do I look
all right?" she asked when he had closed the clasp. By
the time they were ready to leave—she changed her sari
twice because she wanted to look her best at a big gathering of Bengalis—it was too late to take the subway
and Amit grumbled about having to spend unnecessary
money on taxi fare. There were to be two separate cel-
ebrations in the city, arranged by competing factions in
the Bengali community. The Basus were going to the
smaller and more informal *pujah*, which did not involve
any religious rites or heavy subscriptions, but "just a
lot of friends having potluck and seeing an old movie,"
as Vinod Khanna put it. Though Vinod was not a Bengali, he insisted that Bengalis were his favorite people,

and this would be a gift to ''Gotham Bengalis'' by the Khanna Cultural Society. It would be a humble affair in a church basement, but with the right songs, food and even an old Satyajit Ray movie. The other affair was supposed to be much fancier, with a clay goddess Saraswati flown in from Calcutta and an authentic Brahmin priest to recite the prayers and official speeches by office-holders (of the *pujah* committee) and perhaps even a consular official and one of the UN delegates.

''I wonder if they had to pay full airfare for bringing the goddess over,'' Amit said in the taxi on the way over to the church basement near Columbia. But Dimple was too busy smoothing out the gold borders of her Benarasee sari to answer. She wanted people to admire her when she got out of the taxi and followed Amit into the church. She wished she could begin again, forget the six hours she had spent on the park bench in the middle of winter, wanted to look sexy like Ina Mullick who was going to the other *pujah* or perhaps not going at all, and say witty things that would force people to turn around and whisper about her. But she would not begin again, because you could build only on things you had already done. She had learned that simple lesson quite painfully in the last few months and she knew that, while there would be the desire for a hundred new starts, there would never be a real beginning. Sitting in the taxi with the window rolled up, she thought she saw the woman she might have been, a smart woman with pale make-up attending a lecture on Introductory Astrophysics (3 credits): stellar structure . . . neutron stars . . . gravitational collapse . . . she wanted the whole goddamn cosmology made accessible to her. But when the taxi came to a stop and Dimple had to hop from the taxi as gracefully as she could without stepping on the pretty gold border or trailing it in black slushy puddles, the pale lady vanished and thirty plump women in Benarasee saris engulfed her, shouting, "Long time no see, Mrs. Basu. Where have you been hiding lately?" They pulled her wrists, gossiped and laughed; they spilled *kala jamun* syrup on the gold border of Dimple's sari as they jiggled their plates with passion and complained of the price of rice and fish in Calcutta. She watched the black syrup spots eat into the border.

Mrs. Guha, who was dressed in a simple silk sari and wore a pearl choker and matching pearl earrings, said to Dimple, "Do you know they're charging two dollars per head at the other place!"

"That makes it so formal!" cried Mrs. Roy. "I'd rather be informal and have potluck. This is much more fun!"

As Dimple listened to them, she thought that she had judged her marriage too harshly on the day she had walked out of the house in Marsha's silk shirt and Amit's pants, and that here in this large hall with the trestle tables full of food made by Bengali wives like Mrs. Roy and Meena Sen all over Queens and Manhattan, with Vinod Khanna in an embroidered *kurta* giving noisy directions to others and greeting guests in a self-conscious but creditable Bengali, it was possible to revise her opinion, possible to admit that she was happier now than she had been on Dr. Sarat Banerjee Road or even on Rash Behari Avenue, though perhaps not so happy as Pixie was with her actor. She sensed that on the ride back home the pleasant feeling would disappear. She would stare at the cab driver's collar and shoulders through the glass partition and try to avoid his scowling mug-shot looking back at her, and Amit would look out of his window and recite the year and make of passing cars and they would both feel sorry that the *pujah* was over and there would not be another for a whole year.

She heard Mrs. Roy speaking again. "It is true the Mullicks are thinking of going back home?"

"I don't know," Dimple said. "I hadn't heard anything about it. I'm kind of cut off from rumors down in the Village."

"They'll have a hard time adjusting. They've been here too long and they've been too cut off from us," said Meena Sen.

"I don't think so," objected Mrs. Chakladar. "We're all planning to go home when our husbands retire. I mean, who would want to die in Kansas City or something?"

Dimple was not sure where she wanted to die, but she was sure that dying would be just as senseless and unfair in Calcutta; it would be just as horrible and scary to be carried on a flower-strewn bed in a procession, to cause small traffic jams and impatient honking on the streets, to have Amit bend over the corpse (would he cry for her as he bent over?) and hold a torch to her face, wait for it to burst into flames, then step back from the unbearable heat so that his own face and arms would not burn. He would know what to do in Calcutta if she were to die suddenly, but would he cope just as well here in New York if something bad happened to her very suddenly; if for instance, their taxi ran a red light and crashed into a car, would he find an electric crematorium and take good care of her?

The women began shushing each other and Vinod Khanna clapped for attention. When the people in the hall were clumsily quiet—some people even stopped chewing their *samosas* and *pakoras*—Vinod Khanna introduced a little girl with an enormous pink bow in her hair and the little girl belted out two Bengali folk songs in a surprisingly mature voice, and Vinod Khanna led the applause. There were more songs after that, this time by the girl's mother and an economics student at C. W. Post, then the screen was set up in another room for a movie. Amit appeared at Dimple's side during the flow of people from one room to the other and decided it was getting late and that they should not bother to see the film after all.

"But maybe Prosanto Bagchi is acting in this film!" Dimple protested as Amit helped her into her coat and led her out to the sidewalk.

There were no accidents on the way home. Their taxi did not collide with another taxi or car and the taxi driver did not even have his picture behind the front seat. There was only one small incident: Dimple said that she saw two men beating up another man close to their apartment house just as the taxi was slowing down to a stop. Amit told her that she had probably imagined the scene because the papers were so full of muggings and knifings and that a glass of hot milk before bedtime would make her feel well again. Dimple had to agree that she was losing touch with what she saw and what she thought she saw because she had seen it before on television.

She warmed a whole quart of milk and sipped endless mugs, staring at the patterned stars of the World Trade Center. Amit fell asleep on the sofa. But she suffered insomnia.

Between three and four she must have fallen asleep because she dreamed that she was dying. It was a most horrible sensation, not because she was in pain, but because she could see her head, neatly sliced just below the chin, as the base of a pretty table lamp beside the travel alarm clock and a china vase bought at Macy's. She was nothing more than an adumbration.

An after-dream persisted when she woke up: some-one had murdered her the night before and concealed her corpse among the Bedouin brasses and baskets of indoor plants. She wrapped her blue bathrobe tighter around her breasts and hips and did all the things she normally did between seven and eight on weekday mornings, but she knew that she was dead and that Amit would recoil from her as soon as he sat down at the table for his Wheaties and two fried eggs. But when Amit actually emerged from the bedroom in a clean shirt and American suit, his tie still unknotted, all he said was, "Hurry up with the breakfast, can't you? I'll be late for work if you dawdle like that."

After Amit had left, she washed the dishes very slowly because it seemed so nice to let her hands sink into very hot, soapy water, to search for cups, saucers, lids or spoons and knives, mysterious underwater objects, identify them as if she were a marine biologist, stab them with her pink sponge then release them again and feel them float away. It was not at all like washing dishes. But when there were no more dishes left, when she had no choice but to pull out the plug and let the drain suck in the suds in sudden urgent gulps, when the last soap bubble had been washed away and the sink scoured with Ajax, she watered the plants and wiped the leaves. Wiping helped the plants breathe, Milt had said, and she trusted Milt, trusted him so implicitly that she could imagine the leaves sighing their gratitude.

After that she stood under a hot shower, timing it carefully on Marsha's purple alarm clock, which she set on its side among a forest of toothbrushes. In the beginning the water was unbearably hot and the steam made her breathless. She imagined the vapors entering her body and leaving condensation tracks on the inside. Every now and then, very reverently, she touched her skin—she thought of it as the shell she inhabited—

digging aimless red patterns with her fingernails. At the end of forty-seven minutes, when the alarm went off, the vagrant after-dream returned. She had meant the alarm to go off two minutes earlier; it upset her that she still could not master these small things. She was a pitiful immigrant among demanding appliances.

At about eleven-thirty, when she was watering the cactus by the dining-room window for the fourth time, Ina and Milt came in, wearing matching Antartex coats and dark aviator glasses. Their faces were pink with the cold, even Ina's. They laughed, squeezed Dimple's arm in greeting, shook off their scarves and berets and tapped their boots lightly against the umbrella stand. Dimple was happy to see them. These were people who *liked* the cold. She forgave them for leaving slushy crescents on the floor. Ina said they had been "canvasing" in the neighborhood, though both she and Milt were vague about the nature of the work and Dimple was too shy to press for details.

"Amit says one should never discuss politics and religion," Dimple said, smiling and nodding her head. "It always leads to trouble."

Ina's eyes narrowed in venom. She pounced on it as a challenge. "Don't let him bully you!" she cried. Then turning to Milt she added, "We've got to do something for her. Poor old Dimple."

"That's not what I meant," Dimple said quickly. She did not want anything to spoil the morning, especially now that Milt Glasser was here in the apartment and was flinging his coat on the sofa, which meant that he intended to stay a while. Ruses were what she needed: she schemed to render Ina a mute and approving presence. Her desperation concentrated on the drooping cactus in her hand. It had been meant to flower, but now the soil was spotted with fungus.

She held it up to Milt, asked his advice in terrified tones, anticipated his disapproval. "What more does it need? Vitamins? Compost of tea leaves? I've given it all I could." Since the plants belonged to Marsha, Dimple expected him to feel proprietary about them, to scold her for killing so many, even the hardy little ivies and geraniums.

"Love," answered Milt, taking her in his arms, cactus and all. "Like us they respond to love. It's really very simple."

"Leave her alone, Milt," Ina shouted, laughingly. "Dimple, my sweet, accept it. You have basically unsupportive plants." Then she faked a punch at Milt, chased him around the sofa, tripped over his bulky coat and collapsed on the floor, still laughing.

"Sweetheart," Milt began in his Bogart voice, hesitated a few seconds, then switched to his own soft baritone, ". . . I think you are jealous of Dimple." He might have continued if Ina had not thrown a cushion at his head, missed, and knocked down a vase that Marsha had brought back from Jerusalem. Dimple bounded over the sofa to collect the pieces. Ina, still laughing, called, "Did it break? I can pick up a replacement, so don't worry." It hadn't broken. But Dimple thought it would be safer on a bookshelf—Ina and Leni were not readers—because Marsha, mysterious and frightening as she was, deserved better. She decided to hide the cactus also; Marsha's cactus. If she hid it in the kitchen cabinet, high up among the cereal boxes and a stack of paper plates left over from one of Marsha's parties, it could die peacefully, without shame and without reproach. Girls like Ina and Leni broke too many things, Dimple reflected. They didn't kill things the way Dimple did—deliberately, excitedly—and they didn't let things die and things didn't just die on them accidentally

(Dimple was glad she'd not been given Ina's aquarium to preserve; she could imagine those dozens of darting, delicate fish floating belly-up); they killed randomly through some principle of intolerance and profound detachment that Dimple could only think of as American, and beyond her.

"I'll make some tea," Dimple said, moving toward the door with the cactus. "Or coffee, Milt. Would you rather have coffee?"

"Let's have a beer," Ina said. "I'll help you." But she lay stretched out on her back on the shaggy rug, relaxed and very beautiful.

When Dimple returned Milt was on the rug with Ina, and Ina was giving him what she called her "ultimate message" by digging her knuckles and elbows viciously into his back.

"Honey," Milt grunted out of the side of his mouth, his head still buried in the deep pile, "you have the most—ah—articulate elbows I have—eeow!—ever felt."

From the sofa, her island of decency, Dimple said, "Please look out for the pins in that rug. It's very dangerous."

Heedless of the warning, Ina continued to knead untender messages on Milt's flesh. Happy people, Dimple concluded, were capricious, mysterious. She did not expect to understand them, only to listen to their talk. Happy people gravitate; she was not a happy person. But she could imitate them in her dreams, fake punches, tell indecent jokes, walk like a model, be incautious, extravagant, scandalous; no one would know. Amit was not like Milt and Ina. She could not imagine him on the floor, laid out on his stomach, being tickled by a woman.

To show her good faith, Dimple left the shelter of the sofa, walked to the stereo—she had to pass very close to her guests to reach it—and played a Kanika Banerjee LP, and after that a Suchitra Mitra. But the sense of dread that they would go away if she could not entertain them properly remained. "Listen to this part," she urged Milt. "It's terribly poignant. I'll translate it for you." In a choked voice, she continued:

> The road has not come to an end.
> In the dark of the evening
> I cannot see who is walking
> Beside me . . .

She sought a smile, a clue that he had understood. When none came, not even from Ina, she cried a little.

"On the floor, charming lady," Milt ordered in his Indian voice. "You're as tight as a sitar string." Dimple obeyed.

She felt she was missing a mouth or tongue or lips, missing an element necessary to make intelligible noises. Milt did not touch her, not even when Ina moved away to replay the records.

"Tell me that story you started long ago," Dimple said. "I think it must have been last time you were here. You were telling me about the rats and this one brave boy in Harlem."

"I don't remember," he said. "I probably made it up anyway."

It was not possible that he did not remember. She construed his forgetfulness as betrayal. Courage, initiative, that was what the story had promised. Now it was his duty to continue. "Don't you really remember?" she cried, prodding him with her toes. "It was about this boy and his brothers and the rats."

Ina was by the window, humming with Suchitra Mitra. She did not seem depressed or nostalgic.

"You must remember!" Dimple shouted, bringing
her fist down on his back in humorless imitation of Ina.
Her foot—she was surprised to see how it shimmered
in its nylon casing—was poised about his calves, ready
to prod, to hurt and make him scream. The foot frightened her because it seemed capable of independent fury.
"You're teasing me, I know. I will not be teased!
Please, Milt. Out with the story."

Because, Dimple told herself, she *liked* Milt Glasser.
He was the only one she could talk to. With the others,
people like Amit and Ina and even Meena Sen, she
talked in silences. With Milt she could talk about all
sorts of things: clean air acts, emission controls, deple-
tion allowances, the Vinland map forgery, the Knicks
(the year before, Milt had followed them on tour through
New England and the Middle West), Watergate, and
Marilyn Monroe and Mr. Clean and soap operas that
she had started to watch again and the comparative
crunchiness of cereals ("but I like them mushy!" Dimple had said) and it was only toward the end of a conversation that Dimple realized that Milt had done most
of the talking and she most of the listening but that it
had been very exciting all the same. She thought of Milt
as an urban nomad. He was not brilliant and dependable like Amit, but he was easier to talk to though he
was foreign. Sometimes she pressed him to tell her what
he did for a living, but all he would say was that he was
a "consultant" which could mean anything, she supposed, and was probably his way of telling her that she
would not understand, and that made her a little angry.
She had pieced together occasional descriptions so that
she knew his work had something to do with ghetto
children and government spending (she had liked the
sound of that phrase, "government spending"; it made
whatever Milt did sound very professional and impor-

tant). It bothered her that he did not wear suits on
weekdays, like Amit or Bijoy Mullick or Jyoti Sen. How
can one trust a man who did not wear at least a tie and
jacket? He was not like any social worker, though the
only social worker she had ever met had been an Indian
Christian girl who had gone into a village carrying her
posters on family planning and had never been heard
from again. It was hard for Dimple to measure Milt
against a dependable average. He was not fired up with
missionary zeal. He was a solid, even selfish, citizen;
she had seen his billfold once and it was stuffed with
credit cards. Yet she could imagine that a man like Milt,
who pretended to hate the people he worked for and
who made jokes at their expense, could do more real
good for them than a dozen missionaries. And there he
was on the rug, on this cold, miserable day in February,
refusing to talk to her though he knew that she liked to
be talked to, giggling and rolling on the floor while she,
Mrs. Dimple Basu, abused him with her feet and fingernails.

"Well, if no one wants to talk, let's go for a walk,"
Dimple said. Her only regret was that she didn't have
a smart sheepskin coat like Ina's, but she borrowed
Marsha's mauve-tinted glasses to minimize the difference between them.

On the street immediately outside the apartment
complex, Dimple saw a row of cars double-parked and
a smiling cop with his baton jutting out at an angle
under his elbow. A small blue car, which she recognized as a Morris Minor, had four different tickets under its windshield wiper. Its hubcaps were missing.
There were newspapers blowing everywhere. She
thought what a waste of newsprint it was and how her
eyes had hurt in Calcutta trying to read about strikes

and hold-ups because the paper was so brown and smudgy. A large, white, empty bleach bottle rolled with the wind, then fell into the gutter. Farther down the street she saw two kids—they looked so much like Indians they had to be Puerto Ricans—trying to make snowballs from a tiny patch of dusty snow. On the wall of a small playhouse was a poster of a chorus line: twelve black men in blond wigs and military boots. A hatless blond man in a raccoon coat with the collar turned up stood in front of the poster, lighting his cigarette. He had bad skin and teased hair; he was followed by a bald black man and a waist-high Afghan hound.

Ina leered at the Negroes in blond wigs, the bald man walking the dog, and whispered to Dimple, "Wouldn't it be comforting to draw the line somewhere?"

"What do you mean?"

"These Upper West Side types aren't used to the Village," Milt explained.

After that Dimple placed herself between Ina and Milt. They walked past glass storefronts displaying plants, print dresses, candles, leather belts. In one window she saw a candle as tall as herself, shaped like a naked girl. Girls in imitation leather jackets walked in twos; a black man looking for something in a dented garbage can spoke directly to Ina and laughed a lot. Dimple wondered why the cans were so full: paper bags, empty juice and soup cans, celery leaves spilled over the rusty metal tops.

"How about some pizza?" Milt asked.

But Ina said that she had no time for a pizza because she was going to get fitted for contact lenses. "Time for another change of image," she said.

"Better luck next time," said Milt, treating it as a joke while Ina muttered something obscene under her breath. Dimple realized she didn't have the slightest idea of what Ina and Milt thought of each other, or even what they did with each other besides wrestling on the floor and hugging at the door. She didn't even know if Ina and Bijoy were going back to India.

Milt looked at Dimple after Ina turned away and said, "Well, the offer still stands, Dimple. How about a nice little pizza for the two of us?" Then, as she stared at him uncertainly, he broke into a song and dance: "Pizza for two, I and you, Milt and Basu," and so on, rhyming Calcutta with mozzarella, Tagore and bore; one of his relatives, he said, was Irving Berlin. She was amazed that he had no inhibitions: she herself was too afraid even to eat ice cream on the streets during the summer. "Come on, Dimple," he urged, and she yielded to the pressure of his gloved hand rather than to the actual invitation to eat a pizza. She was amazed and horrified to see herself soft-shoeing her way with Milt over to the nearby pizzeria. "Dimple, Dimple, Dimple!" he was singing. "I love to say that name." She felt it was not Dimple Basu who was singing and giggling with Milt Glasser.

At the pizzeria, Milt told a long story that involved Milt himself and the management of Madison Square Garden, where he'd failed an interview for the job of usher (a good thing, he admitted, since he'd never have gone on to college if he'd had a nightly pass to the Knicks and Rangers). Dimple decided she could explain the guilty adventure to Amit in two ways. She could pretend that she had been taken against her will to the pizzeria, maybe even pretend that Ina Mullick had left to be fitted after lunch rather than before, and play Milt as a believably inoffensive younger brother of a friend—an American Pintu. Or she could convince herself that she had not gone out with Milt, because to go unwillingly was not to go at all. That way she would have nothing to explain to Amit. Eating a pizza, was, after all, a very small crime and should not require too great an explanation. The main thing was to convince herself that Milt had forced her into the pizzeria.

Sitting at the table, she kept worrying about what the waiter thought of her. He had a vengeful face and hair in his ears. Like Amit, he was an old man in his late twenties.

"Dimple," Milt said again. Subtly different: the word, not her name.

"Yes?"

"Nothing," Milt answered, smiling.

The waiter walked between tables, restless, grim, carrying nothing. She wished he would go away. He had no right to make her feel guilty. Milt was a nice person, impulsive and frank. Besides, he was Marsha Mookerji's brother, guardian spirit of the plants. Amit could not object to her having a pizza with him.

When Milt called for the check (which he did without raising a finger, just a slight up-and-down motion of the neck) she realized again how different he was from Amit. Amit did not like eating out in New York and the one time they had gone out for fried chicken, the waiter had kept him deliberately waiting though there had been only one other couple in the restaurant. She had wanted to scream, sitting patiently with a mustached man snapping his fingers. Exchange of money embarrassed her; it was a manly ritual, so she folded and refolded her grease-spotted paper napkin and devised a third way to deal with guilt. She would kill Amit and hide his body in the freezer. The extravagance of the scheme delighted her, made her feel very American somehow, almost like a character in a TV series. Amit's tragedy was that he lacked extravagance; he persevered in the immigrant virtues of caution and cunning.

She watched Milt leave a tip, walk toward the back of the restaurant where the bathrooms were (in her reconstructions there were no bathrooms and she thought it unfair of Milt to use one now). To avoid the waiter's stare, she moved to the front door, staying just inside. She dreamed up extravagant details: the small parts, the fingers, tonsils, heart and gizzard could be packed in plastic bags. Housework could be *creative* and *challenging*; she tried to think of the other words that Amit had written on his list when he had been job-hunting.

In a few minutes, Milt, enormous in his coat, loomed beside her and the tufted waiter brought her a handkerchief that she had left behind, and Milt said that he would walk her back but that he had to vamoose at three o'clock because he had an appointment with his "project assessor."

So Milt Glasser took Dimple home. He walked quickly, and by the time they had reached the policeman still ticketing cars, she was breathing hard and lagging behind. Milt paused long enough to mutter something to the policeman who snorted tolerantly, though he did not stop making out tickets. "He used to pound a beat in my uncle's old neighborhood in the Bronx," Milt explained, and Dimple was amazed again that in the hands of Milt Glasser, the inhuman maze of New York became as safe and simple as Ballygunje. When they reached the elevator, Dimple asked him to please come up and unlock the front door for her because she had trouble with Marsha's key; no matter how she jiggled it, it always got stuck.

"It shouldn't take more than a minute or two. I know you're in a hurry."

He preceded her into the elevator and then down the

hall. When she had trouble finding her key in her purse
(perhaps she had dropped it in the pizzeria), he opened
the door to the apartment with his own key.

"Now that you've lured me up here, you might as
well make me your famous Darjeeling tea. And then
I'll be off."

Dimple took Milt's coat, grateful that he was staying.
The coat was still warm, and the sleeves jutted from
the sides, still retaining the shape of Milt's arms. She
put it carefully in the hall closet next to Amit's Barkat
Ali suit. Smiling her consent, she said, "Okay, Milt,
I'll make you my Darjeeling Special."

An hour later she thought that for a tall person Milt
Glasser had very short legs. On the whole, he was hairy;
he had hair all over his body, on his chest, shoulders,
thighs and even on the bulges of his calf muscles. He
was very muscular, especially in the legs, which came
from basketball, he said. Amit was hairy on the face,
and not at all muscular. Amit shaved at night before
going to bed, and again in the morning, "just to make
sure," he always said. And he would not wear blue
bikini briefs and sit on the sofa reading the papers if he
had an appointment to keep at three o'clock. Dimple
had considered the three o'clock appointment her protection: it had turned out to be a trigger. She did not
think that Amit would wear bikini briefs under any circumstances.

She sat self-consciously on the sofa, straightening
cushions and running her fingernails over the corduroy
ridges, trying to figure out a satisfying ending. In the
bedroom she had kept her eyes shut. But the living room
was wrong, undignified, quite unsuitable for lovers (if
that's what they were now). A heroic effort had kept her
from getting fully dressed again. She was in her bra
and long cotton petticoat and Marsha's tinted glasses:

it was almost like being naked. It was essential that the glasses did not come off a second time even if the bra and petticoat did. The glasses were part of her disguise. She could look through the purple lenses at Milt Glasser's briefs and still not be embarrassed. If you plan your moves right, she thought, you could still become anything you wanted to: Prosanto Bagchi's wife, Ping-Pong champion of your state, lover of a genuine American. But Ping-Pong was out of her reach now; she had no state to represent and she had failed to re-create a new one in the limits of her apartment as Meena or Ina or Mrs. Roy had done. Under ideal conditions she should have been wearing a lacy little bra (Marsha's drawers were stuffed with them), but life never seemed to provide ideal circumstances. She wondered what she looked like to Milt as she sat with her ankles neatly crossed, poised on what she called "the very brink of crisis." She wondered why she was so obsessed by Amit's phrases, especially since they sounded absurd whenever he tried to use them.

Milt was reading the newspaper. She wanted to jolt him, accidentally, of course, so that he could witness her agony. He had no right to read the paper and spoil beautiful endings.

Dimple looked over his shoulder—the skin was very white under the dark hair—and tried to read the paper with him, without worrying about the jagged tear in her petticoat. It was an old petticoat. She had bought it three years before in the New Market and Pixie had bargained with the old Muslim shop assistant in an embroidered cap and brought the price down from nine-fifty to six-fifty-five. If she could have planned this scene days in advance she would have mended the tear in the petticoat and looked for a more wispy bra.

The newspaper told of a girl in Los Angeles who had

been shot twice in the chest in front of a laundromat. The girl was called Mickie Malka and she would have been twenty-five if she had lived one more day. There was a picture of Mickie Malka on the sidewalk; her head was out of focus. Her left leg was bent at the knee; on her right foot was a chunky shoe. The faces of the policemen were clearer. Two crouched beside the body and seemed to be fiddling with buttons on the jacket (Dimple assumed the smudgy black spots in the picture were blood, because there were many black spots on the blouse). Two others, guns in view, stood behind the body, in reflective poses. There was also an un-uniformed black man in a patterned jacket, chewing the tip of his tie and talking to someone outside the picture.

"Is that a police officer in mufti?" Dimple asked. "Or is that the lover? There's always a romantic angle in your American murders."

"Bunch a crazies," Milt said through his teeth and tapped the picture with his fingernail. "Dimple, promise you won't ever go to California. That's for starts." He wrapped his enormous arm around her cold shoulders; it was a cool, protective arm, though she couldn't draw any closer to his body. "Dimple, I'd like to look after you. You need some looking after."

She could feel his arm sweating; she could smell the sweat and wondered if it would go away before Amit came home.

"I'm not good at this kind of talk, Dimple. I'm good at every other kind of talk, but not this. But I want you to know I'm not just a dumb jock and I'm not just Marsha Glasser's brother and I'm not just hustling the foundations. Sometimes I'm halfway serious about things."

It seemed the right time. She could ask him now. "Do you mind if I ask you something personal?"

He snickered. "I have no secrets from you, not now. What is it—about Ina?"

"Milt? What kind of work do you really do? I mean, you must be pretty important if you're involved with government spending and project assessors."

Milt stared into his newspaper. "*That's* your personal question? Here I am thinking I'll kidnap you to protect you from all the crazies—I'm even thinking you want me to stick around when that husband of yours comes walking through the door, and I'm telling myself, okay, I'll even do that—for her. And there's no love like that kind of love. And you want to know about my job. My job!"

"Please," she said desperately, "I know I didn't say it right. I want to know you better. How can I know you if I don't know your job? Would you like another cup of tea?"

"Yes, I'd like more tea. Go make more tea, Dimple." He patted her bottom as she bounced out of the room in her torn petticoat and no-nonsense bra.

In the kitchen, where she had not worked in near nudity before, she thought of a new way to die. Go to the laundry room in the basement after midnight and hang around the machines in bra and petticoat, behind dark glasses. She knew she had mismanaged it all; she'd seen enough TV and read enough novels to know this was the time to lie in bed, to hum little songs, to pinch, pull, slap; it was not the time to reach for dark glasses and sensible undergarments and make discreet inquiries about the young man's job. She was so much worse off than ever, more lonely, more cut off from Amit, from the Indians, left only with borrowed disguises. She felt like a shadow without feelings. Whatever she did, no matter how coolly she planned it, would be wrong.

Milt stood fully dressed by the kitchen door; he was

running his hands through his curly hair. She handed him his cup of tea, which he sipped while standing. "I'm sorry for what I said. You shocked me, that's all. Everything about you is shocking and exciting and a little sad." He slurped very loudly, like a Bengali. "Dimple, you're the most gorgeous creature in New York—did anyone ever tell you that? But it's two-thirty and I've got promises to keep or I'll be out on my ass. Ciao, Dimple."

"Don't be sorry," Dimple whispered. "I never expected life to be a bed of cherries."

After he left, she noticed that his teacup was still half full. She cushioned her head in her arms and wept.

"Well, how about it," Amit asked that evening.

"How about what?"

"I *knew* it! I caught you. God! It's like talking to a deaf-mute and it's getting worse every day."

"I was listening," Dimple protested. "I just didn't get the last part."

"Then you should be able to guess the last part. It should be pretty obvious if you were listening to the rest of it."

"You never listen to my advice anyway, so why ask me these questions?"

"I think I'll shave it off," Amit said. "No one else has a mustache in the office. I'll feel less conspicuous if I shave."

Dimple wrote a letter to Miss Problem-Walla:

Question:
How can I tell if I'm really in love? I've met this boy who is not of my caste and class and my heart tells me it is love but how can I be sure? I have met him several times, and once under rather in-

timate circumstances, the memory of which still makes me blush somewhat. He is rather unconventional and nonconformist, you might say. I have enquired into his family background: his father is the athletic type and his mother is ailing (she has piles, also ulcers). They are both retired people. The problem is that he hasn't actually expressed his love for me to me. He is a very generous-hearted person. The reason I know this is because a friend of mine, also an Indian resident here, has spoken very affectionately of him. Whenever I think of him, my heart dances a jig and there is an uncomfortable though exciting feeling in my throat. Is love to be measured by physiological symptoms? Please help me, for I cannot ascertain if this is really love. I just cannot.

D. B.New York

Two weeks later Miss Problem-Walla wrote back saying that she handled beauty problems only and that if Miss Basu had any worries regarding dry skin, limp hair, puckered thighs, etcetera, she would be glad to help in any way she could.

Because she had enjoyed it, Dimple thought, she would not do it again. She would not complicate her life. Clumsy people should not lead complicated lives. She would not confide in anyone because that would complicate the problem.

Milt Glasser did not call for over a week. Then on a Tuesday morning he came to the apartment with tickets for a show. He said that the show was called *The Bull's Eye* and would star one of his high-school buddies. His friend would run around in circles in Madison Square

Garden while spectators threw darts, javelins and ar-
rows at him. The idea was very profound, Milt explained, though easily corrupted. It had to do with
redeeming a society poisoned with violence. Conceiv-
ably, it could feed the violence; it was intended to es-
trange the audience from violence. A distant cousin had
the bow-and-arrow concession.

"That's art?" Dimple asked.

Milt talked animatedly about audience involvement
and she remembered that she had once felt he was the
only person she could talk to. Now she was not listening to his words so much as memorizing his gestures
and mannerisms, because she had a premonition that
she would not see him again. She was almost sure that
he had invented the show called *The Bull's Eye* and
that there were no tickets in his pocket. She served him
four cups of tea, with lemon and sugar because the milk
had gone sour (the milk had gone sour because she had
left it out since Amit went to work at seven-thirty), and
wondered if he was wearing blue bikini briefs again.
She did not ask to see the tickets. "Watch out, Milt
Glasser," she said bitterly after he had left the apartment. Tuesdays, according to her horoscope, were
unlucky days.

Mrs. Dasgupta wrote that Calcutta was having an unusual cold spell and that temperatures were running 2°C
below normal quite consistently, and that there had been
power cuts nearly every other day, and a strike over
rising prices and a demonstration about God knew what
and a bus had been almost burned very close to their
house and wasn't she lucky not to have to worry about
such problems. Further down the letter, Dimple read
that Pixie had a lovely flat on Lord Sinha Road and *two*
refrigerators in her kitchen, and that her father had de-

veloped mild diabetes and had been put on a strict diet. Pixie had brought Prosanto Bagchi over for tea, and they were pleased to report he was an *extremely* charming man, who turned out to be from the same district in East Bengal as Mr. Dasgupta's mother. And later still: If you can come to India this summer on a charter flight, please try to come. I hear that charter flights are not expensive and you can stay up to four months maximum. We are missing you very much as usual. Your father sends his blessings. Then she had added as a postscript: Can you bring a transistor radio for your father? He has always wanted one. He will pay Amit in *rupees* when you get here.

Meena Sen called Dimple. She was still looking for a name for the new baby. "My mother-in-law suggests Alokananda or Dipali. So we'll have to come up very quickly with a better name."

"You're sure you don't like Alokananda? You could get used to it. I can't think of anything at all. My head feels so empty. I guess I'm getting one of my bad headaches."

"But I hate Alokananda. We've got to do better than that. I have eight Bengali wives working on names right now. Call me back when your headache goes away."

"I can tell I'm in for a three-day headache."

"We need something that's short and simple. You know, something that won't sound *too* odd here; but it has to be very Bengali all the same. What about Reeta?"

"Don't worry," Dimple said as she got ready to hang up. "No one ever stays nameless. The baby will get a name."

"I know the name she'll get. That's the whole trouble. If I can't think of something at once, they'll all start calling her Alokananda.''

"I'm terrible in crises," Dimple said.

She felt very low, as if she might come down with flu, but there was no fever, not even a cold. It would have been better if the thermometer had registered some abnormality. Then she could have said, "I'm ill. I must take two aspirins, drink plenty of fluids and rest in bed." Television had taught her to cope with life's *real* problems. But it was the imaginary ills that were impossible to treat. She felt moody and lightheaded.

The after-dream returned. Only this time her head was like a Lucite paperweight. She could see her brain, pinkish and plump, pressing against the sides, trying to escape. She panicked; the image was intolerable, indecent. Well-brought up girls did not indulge in such excesses. But there it was, and the more she concentrated, the clearer the image became, until the pink blob she had taken to be her brain turned out to be an animal instead, a miniature animal, perfectly and fully developed with its own digestive and respiratory systems; in fact, a fetal rhinoceros trapped in a decorative paperweight. She remembered something that Mrs. Basu had said before she and Amit were married: that Dimple was too dark, that she was not the Basus' first choice.

Meena Sen called again, and Dimple broke down and told her she was suffering from insomnia and headaches.

"It's homesickness," Meena Sen said. "If you were in Queens, you wouldn't feel so lost. You could drop in for tea anytime at my place or Mrs. Roy's. She's a nice woman."

"Maybe we could move when the Mookerjis come back."

"But how do you like the name Nandini?" Meena asked.

"I'll call you back when I feel better. Maybe later tonight," Dimple said and hung up.

Amit watched the Johnny Carson show in the bedroom because he could not sleep. Dimple sneered because he did not seem to know rule number one about insomnia: it did not begin until three A.M. If Amit was not asleep by eleven-thirty, it was insomnia. He'd never been awake after one-fifteen in his life. Johnny Carson wore an enormous turban and answered funny questions in an Indian accent. The faucet dripped in the kitchen sink and made a soft, popping noise. Whenever Johnny Carson stopped talking, the faucet started. "It's the washer, probably," Amit said to Dimple. They didn't know how to fix it; in any case it was the Mookerjis' faucet.

From the bedroom window Dimple could see the gas station. Its handwritten sign said: SORRY, FOLKS. WE'RE OUT OF GAS. A woman with long blond hair and satin pants said, "Yes, dahling, we built a raft with our own hands!" She held up her hands for the TV cameras and Johnny tried to kiss them. There is no sign there, Dimple thought. How can I see a sign there when I'm short-sighted? Johnny said, "Yes, folks. There's a man holding up a sign here that says KISS HAND. The man's wearing sequined sideburns." There were cars at the gas station: a long line of cars that snaked around the pumps and trailed off into the urban wilderness. Any minute now, Dimple thought, someone's going to get out of his car and shoot someone else. Sure enough, a fat man in a green windbreaker got out of his Chevelle and shot a thin man hiding behind a pump. There was blood all over the thin man's Exxon overalls and there was a male chorus of gas attendants bending over the corpse like policemen. Goddamnit, thought Dimple, when you get television mixed up with real life you're very near the end.

"I don't want to start on sleeping pills," Amit said to Dimple. A young man who wore his curly hair like Milt Glasser's was talking about suicide. His profile was angular; the rest of him was like a wrestler in evening clothes. "I think he's wearing tight underwear," Dimple said. Amit was shocked. "No," he said, "sleeping pills destroyed this chap. He admits as much." Amit stretched his hand for the bowl of peanuts and discovered there were only four. "What do you do all day? Eat peanuts and sleep?" The young wrestler in tight underwear said that his parents had always been against him, that they had broken a Rolling Stones album when he had been fifteen. "Do you mean that when your parents took away your Rolling Stones album, you had your first impulse to kill them?" asked a middle-aged woman in tuxedo and cummerbund. "You might say that was when I had my *last* impulse," smiled the young man. "Goodness gracious, how can Johnny let him say such things?" Dimple demanded. "I'm sure Johnny won't like that."

"How can you eat peanuts all day?" Amit demanded.

"I don't," Dimple said.

A tall black woman in a white evening cape moved from her swivel chair to a little stage decorated with gigantic wooden crates. She sat on a crate and shed her evening cape.

"Wo-oh-oh-oh," the woman sang.

"They're so musical, aren't they?" Dimple remarked. The wo-oh-oh-oh jarred her body, shocking but not entirely unpleasant, and in the impact some tiny sliver seemed to detach itself and float before her, like visible breath on winter days. Amit was sitting next to her ("Oh, God! I'm going to be dead on my feet tomorrow!" he kept complaining) but the strange sensation persisted. To calm herself, she asked him, "Would tea help? I can make you a cup in two minutes."

"No," Amit snapped. "It would keep me awake. I wish this one would shut up now, because the last two are supposed to be really great." "Woh-ohh-ohh-man!" the black singer exploded.

The sensation was still there: something had torn loose and was hanging, *in space*, while she, Dimple Basu, sat demurely in bed with her husband. Feet together, palms crossed on lap, like ancestors composing serene faces for the photographer and posterity. "Don't you like the way I make tea?" she demanded. "Everyone else does."

"I think this lady is just about to quit, thank goodness. Come on, come on, hurry it up."

"Woh-oh-oh-man," the singer breathed into the microphone wrapping the cord around her chest.

"I don't feel right," Dimple said. "There's something wrong with my head."

"Is it all stuffed up? Take two aspirins and go to bed."

"No," she said, inching closer to him so that only a pillow remained between them. "It's not that . . . it's just that you . . ." She groped for the right words, then remembering Ina and Milt, she pounced on an English word and trotted it out the way Ina had done on a more eventful day. "You just aren't *supportive*, if you know what I mean."

"You're nuts," Amit retorted. But he took his notebook out of his pajama pocket and scribbled down a word.

Dimple tried to sidle closer to him so she could make out what he had written. Could he be writing down *her* word, adding it to his list of words to show off in company? Revenge! Revenge! She watched him slide the notebook back into his pocket, then resume his stiff position. Two people lying stiffly in the Mookerjis' bed, watching Johnny Carson on the Mookerjis' TV. We're only paying rent, Dimple told herself.

The man who looked like Milt kissed the black singer. Dimple could feel the shudder in Amit's arm. The man asked if she had ever jumped from a fifteenth floor window. And been saved, Johnny added. People shouldn't go around saving other people, the man said.

"If I tried to commit suicide, would you save me?" Dimple asked.

"I'm sure you'd bungle it," Amit laughed. "There'd be no need for me to save you. You'd save yourself."

"That's the operable word," said a very thin man with teased blond hair. Dimple was sure she'd seen him on Bleecker Street. "I dare my wife to electrocute me in the bath water, I dare my best friend to shoot me in the chest, but they can't do it. They're afraid."

"What's the operable word?" Dimple asked.

"I don't know. He's a nothing. Let's hope the next guy is better."

The next man was dark, with a very large head and a tiny body. At first she thought it was a child, but when she looked closely, it turned out to be a man in his early thirties. The funny thing was that he looked a bit like Amit in spite of the large head. He held a birdcage in his hand. The cage was empty but the man talked as if there were a bird in it. Johnny did a polite combination of being bewildered and being amused.

"Is he crazy?" Dimple asked.

"Just shut up and listen," Amit said. "He's supposed to be really great."

"Is he or is he not holding an empty birdcage?"

"What are you talking about?" Amit asked. "This is the Italian sailor who sailed on the raft with that black singer and the blond starlet. Just listen to this bit; listen to what happened in the Bay of Bengal!"

But the birdcage was there and now it had a small thing suspended from its swing, a hairy thing with a baby face; she could not be sure whose face since all baby faces were the same. She had to get out of there; she had to save herself. Not that it was uncomfortable: there was a bowl of water and birdseed and the swing was a lot of fun, if you liked to swing, and she could remember having been happy in spite of the striped shadow of the bars because happiness was mostly a shadowy place and sleep.

Someone poked the small feathery thing in the cage. It was Johnny and he wore his enormous turban and blue bikini briefs. He held a stick in his hand, the kind that doctors and dentists used in ads to point to words on charts. He poked and poked the baby face till it was a mangled, bleeding mess.

"So that's the kind of person who wears bikini briefs?" Dimple said.

The dark man took out the bloody, feathered thing and wrapped it in newspaper that he had thoughtfully brought to the show and put the package in his pocket. Then, to show there were no hard feelings, he took the paper from his pocket, pulled one end, and extracted two silk scarves, two rabbits and one wispy bra.

* * *

As soon as Johnny said good night to Amit and Dimple, Amit said, "I'm going to have a bowl of Wheaties. Then let's go over our monthly budget. You're spending too much on cleaning fluids and pesticides and cake mixes and useless items like that. We're not running a hospital, for God's sake. Come out to the kitchen."

Dimple wondered if this was a good time to tell him that she had seduced Milt Glasser and that if it had not been for the project assessor—there was always an assessor lurking in the dead ends of her life—she might have been sleeping with Milt on a regular basis, like some of the wives on soap operas, and leading an exciting double life and nearing a bad end. Amit was in the living room, crossing the shaggy rug to turn off a lamp. On the soap operas, infidelity always led to pregnancy, abortion, murder and blackmail; except that in the past few months she had watched so much television that she knew how to cope with crises like that.

"*Arré!* What the hell!" came Amit's roar from the living room. She raced out of the bedroom to find him hopping on one foot in the middle of the living room, then falling back onto the sofa. "I went to turn off that goddamn light and now look—" He held the foot out to her, and she could see a needle, embedded nearly to its eye, projecting from the soft wrinkled arch of his foot. A fine thread of blood trickled from the puncture.

"I will pull it straight out," she said, and grabbing the needle firmly, extracted it without pain, without further bleeding. It had not broken off, had not blunted itself against a bone. Amit blamed her for the needle in the rug, and to show his independence, refused to let her put on the Band-Aid. When he returned from the bathroom he sat himself at the kitchen table.

It was only the pre-infidelity stage that was difficult, she'd learned, because there were no rules for that phase. Individual initiative, that's what it came down to, and her life had been devoted only to pleasing others, not herself. Amit had no idea how close she had come to betraying him completely and not just paying the price for too much fear and loneliness.

He was standing by the counter when she came into the kitchen. Without turning around he said, ''We should have more potatoes and less frozen broccoli. You're too extravagant. The important thing is I've been working seven months and we haven't even saved a thousand dollars.''

She noticed the Wheaties flakes on the counter. And sugar—he always spilled sugar on the counter. It was one of the little things that irritated her. She thought how horrible to have to spend a whole lifetime watching him spill sugar on counters, how many pounds of wasted sugar that would add up to in thirty years or forty years; but he never thought of such things, never thought how hard it was for her to keep quiet and smile though she was falling apart like a very old toy that had been played with, sometimes quite roughly, by children who claimed to love her.

She opened and closed the kitchen drawer, and heard Amit put a spoonful of cereal in his mouth and whirl it noisily around and under his tongue, then release it for further passage down to the stomach by swallowing forcefully. She sneaked up on him and chose a spot, her favorite spot just under the hairline, where the mole was getting larger and browner, and she drew an imaginary line of kisses because she did not want him to think she was the impulsive, foolish sort who acted like a maniac just because the husband was suffering from insomnia. She touched the mole very lightly and let her fingers draw a circle around the delectable spot, then she brought her right hand up and with the knife stabbed the magical circle once, twice, seven times, each time a little harder, until the milk in the bowl of cereal was a pretty pink and the flakes were mushy and would have embarrassed any advertiser, and then she saw the head fall off—but of course it was her imagination because she was not sure anymore what she had seen on TV and what she had seen in the private screen of three A.M.—and it stayed upright on the counter top, still with its eyes averted from her face, and she said very loudly to the knife that was redder now than it had ever been when she had chopped chicken and mutton with it in the same kitchen and on the same counter, "I wonder if Leni can make a base for it; she's supposed to be very clever with her fingers."

Women on television got away with murder.

About the Author

Bharati Mukherjee was born in Calcutta and lived in Toronto and Montreal before moving to the United States. She attended college in India and earned her doctorate from the University of Iowa. She is the author of three collections of short stories, two works of nonfiction, and two other novels. She has taught creative writing at Columbia, NYU, and Queens College, and she currently holds a distinguished professorship at Berkeley. She and her husband, fellow writer Clark Blaise, have two grown sons.

BHARATI

MUKHERJEE

"Superbly delineates the tensions and contradictions encountered by these (today's) new Americans... an unusual angle of vision on the immigrant dream..."

Boston Herald